A Modest Proposal

JONATHAN SWIFT

A Modern Proposal

ABEL PRUDHOMME

Both *A Modest Proposal,* by Jonathan Swift and *A Modern Proposal,* by Abel Prudhomme contain works of satirical fiction in which names, characters, places, and incidents are the products of the authors' imaginations or are used fictitiously. Any resemblance to actual events, locales, or persons, living or dead, is entirely coincidental.

Copyright © 2012, 2014 Abel Prudhomme

All rights reserved. No part of this publication may be reproduced, distributed, or transmitted in any form or by any means, including photocopying, recording, or other electronic or mechanical methods, without the prior written permission of the publisher, except in the case of brief quotations embodied in critical reviews and certain other noncommercial uses permitted by copyright law. For permission requests, please submit correspondence to

Ross M Ross Publishing
"Attention: Permissions Coordinator"
via the website listed below.

www.abelprudhomme.com

Ordering Information:
Quantity sales. Special discounts are available on quantity purchases by corporations, associations, and others. For details, contact the publisher at the address above.
Orders by U.S. trade bookstores and wholesalers. Please contact Ross M Ross Publishing: Tel: (626) 394-2639; or visit www.abelprudhomme.com.
Seminars and speaking engagement. Abel. Prudhomme is available for public speaking engagement through the contact information given above.

Printed in the United States of America

ISBN-13: 978-1493616435
ISBN-10: 1493616439

Second Edition

14 12 / 10 9 8 7 6 5 4 3 2 1

All rights reserved.

DEDICATION

To my first born son, Jason Johan Prudhomme, a great American.

CONTENTS

A Modest Proposal (and other short satirical works), by Jonathan Swift

    Acknowledgments

    Introduction

1	A Modest Proposal	Pg 1
2	Judas	Pg 13
3	A Digression on … Wars and Quarrels	Pg 15
4	To Quilca, a Country House Not in Good …	Pg 19
5	A Meditation Upon a Broomstick	Pg 21
6	Thoughts on Various Subjects	Pg 25
7	A Satirical Elegy	Pg 37
8	An Argument Against Abolishing Christianity	Pg 41
9	The Day of Judgement	Pg 55

A Modern Proposal (and other brief related works), by Abel Prudhomme

1	A Modern Proposal	Pg 1
2	A Civil Rights Anthem	Pg 7
3	Proposal #1: End the Death Camps	Pg 9
4	How Much Does a Planet Cost?	Pg 15
5	Proposal #2: End Global Suicide	Pg 17
6	Her Khan	Pg 31
7	Proposal #3: Wake Up!	Pg 35

8	*A Trilogy of Short Satire*	
	I. Lyre, Lyre, Forest on Fire!	Pg 45
	II. What Was I Thinking?	Pg 48
	III. Save the Martians!	Pg 50

9	Tree	Pg 53
	About the Authors	Pg 63

ACKNOWLEDGMENTS

A tip of the hat, a bow of the head, an unspoken "couldn't have done it without you" to all who beheld the snatches of time. Your encouragements are translated here. A heartfelt thanks to my mentors on this project: Lisa Moreno, Ann Warren, Nuala Lincke-Ivic, John Tabakian, and Cal Liedtke, who were all so delightfully entertained. To Dr. R. L. Hymers, Jr., Pastor, friend, father, great instrument of who I am, you re-acquainted me with my native tongue, English, new *and* old, yet I shall forever thank you for much more. Lastly, and across the dimensions of time, I am compelled to speak. Mr. Jonathan Swift, odd fellows though we be, this is now our book! I apologize for the lack of collaboration, but we can talk as long as you like when we finally meet.

INTRODUCTION

Gulliver's Travels is not just a children's book about tiny little people tying a full grown man to the ground. It is rather, one of the greatest and most daring satires ever written in the English language.. but not the best! That moniker, in the vast span of literary history, is solely afforded to another of Jonathan Swift's famous works; one properly and fully known as, *A Modest Proposal For Preventing the Children of Poor People in Ireland from Being a Burden on Their Parents or Country, and for Making Them Beneficial to the Public.* A work popularly and simply remembered as **A Modest Proposal.**

It is almost impossible to stop reading once plunged into the opening satirical tirade against certain "beggars of the female sex." Compellingly written during the early 1700s, Swift's tiny little essay, with uncanny wit and precision, immediately unmasked the hypocrisy of the British elite *and* became the very literature that spearheaded a movement against them. Swift wrote other satirical works that balance out his revelation of an imbalanced world and its need for restoration. Many of these are also made available in this edition.

Now, 300 years later, the heart of the American elite is even more darkly set against the less fortunate in *their* midst. More frightening still is the fact that the answer then comically suggested by Swift is a horrifying future into which our world could easily slide.

A Modern Proposal for What To Do with Illegal Immigrants, Welfare Recipients and the Reproduction of Their Children takes the spirit of Swift's revelation and applies it to today. A direct and aggressively humorous update to this truth returned, it likewise rips the tainted veil from the face of a polluted bride. However, **A Modern Proposal**, after its very properly applied satire, goes beyond the realm of complaint to deliver three startling propositions. Song, story, rhyme, and an action packed poem also help to lead the way towards the sanity of a reclaimed world.

Can it be done? Read! Decide! Clink your glass to ignorance… or rise and put an end to the consequences to come!

A

Modest

Proposal

(and other short satirical works)

by

Jonathan

Swift

"…and I believe no gentleman would repine to give ten shillings for the carcass of a good fat child…"

A MODEST PROPOSAL

For preventing the children of poor people in Ireland from being a burden on their parents or country, and for making them beneficial to the public.

Jonathan Swift

1729

It is a melancholy object to those, who walk through this great town, or travel in the country, when they see the streets, the roads and cabin-doors crowded with beggars of the female sex, followed by three, four, or six children, all in rags, and importuning every passenger for alms. These mothers instead of being able to work for their honest livelihood, are forced to employ all their time in strolling to beg sustenance for their helpless infants who, as they grow up, either turn thieves for want of work, or leave their dear native country, to fight for the Pretender in Spain, or sell themselves to the Barbados.

I think it is agreed by all parties, that this prodigious number of children in the arms, or on the backs, or at the heels of their mothers, and frequently of their fathers, is in the present deplorable state of the kingdom, a very great additional grievance; and therefore whoever could find out a fair, cheap and easy method of making these children sound and useful members of the common-wealth, would deserve so well of the public, as to have his statue set up for a preserver of the nation.

But my intention is very far from being confined to provide only for the children of professed beggars: it is of a much greater extent, and shall take in the whole number of infants at a certain age, who are born of parents in effect as little able to support them, as those who demand our charity in the streets.

As to my own part, having turned my thoughts for many years, upon this important subject, and maturely weighed the several schemes of our projectors, I have always found them grossly mistaken in their computation. It is true, a child just dropped from its dam, may be supported by her milk, for a solar year, with little other nourishment: at most not above the value of two shillings, which the mother may certainly get, or the value in scraps, by her lawful occupation of begging; and it is exactly at one year old that I propose to provide for them in such a manner, as, instead of being a charge upon their parents, or the parish, or wanting food and raiment for the rest of their lives, they shall, on the contrary, contribute to the feeding, and partly to the clothing of many thousands.

There is likewise another great advantage in my scheme, that it will prevent those voluntary abortions, and that horrid practice of women murdering their bastard children, alas! too frequent among us, sacrificing the poor innocent babes, I doubt, more to avoid the expense than the shame, which would move tears and pity in the most savage and inhuman breast.

The number of souls in this kingdom being usually reckoned one million and a half, of these I calculate there may be about two hundred thousand couple whose wives are breeders; from which number I subtract thirty thousand couple, who are able to maintain their own children, (although I apprehend there cannot be so many, under the present distresses of the kingdom) but this being granted, there will remain an hundred and seventy thousand breeders. I again subtract fifty thousand, for those women who miscarry, or whose children die by accident or disease within the year. There only remain an hundred and twenty thousand children of poor parents annually born. The question therefore is, how this number shall be reared, and provided for? Which, as I have already said, under the present situation of affairs, is utterly impossible by all the methods hitherto proposed. For we can neither employ them in handicraft or agriculture; we neither build houses, (I mean in the country) nor cultivate land: they can very seldom pick up a livelihood by stealing till they arrive at six years old; except where they are of promising parts, although I confess they learn the rudiments much earlier; during which time they can however be properly looked upon only as probationers: As I have been informed by a principal gentleman in the county of Cavan, who protested to me, that he never knew above one or two instances under the age of six, even in a part of the kingdom so renowned for the quickest proficiency in that art.

I am assured by our merchants, that a boy or a girl before twelve years old, is no saleable commodity, and even when they come to this age, they will not yield above three pounds, or three pounds and half a crown at most, on the exchange; which cannot turn to account either to the parents or kingdom, the charge of nutriments and rags having been at least four times that value.

I shall now therefore humbly propose my own thoughts, which I hope will not be liable to the least objection.

I have been assured by a very knowing American of my acquaintance in London, that a young healthy child well nursed, is, at a year old, a most delicious nourishing and wholesome food, whether stewed, roasted, baked, or boiled; and I make no doubt that it will equally serve in a fricassee, or a ragout.

I do therefore humbly offer it to public consideration, that of the hundred and twenty thousand children, already computed, twenty thousand may be reserved for breed, whereof only one fourth part to be males; which is more than we allow to sheep, black cattle, or swine, and my reason is, that these children are seldom the fruits of marriage, a circumstance not much regarded by our savages, therefore, one male will be sufficient to serve four females. That the remaining hundred thousand may, at a year old, be offered in sale to the persons of quality and fortune, through the kingdom, always advising the mother to let them suck plentifully in the last month, so as to render them plump, and fat for a good table. A child will make two dishes at an entertainment for friends, and when the family dines alone, the fore or hind quarter will make a reasonable dish, and seasoned with a little pepper or salt, will be very good boiled on the fourth day, especially in winter.

I have reckoned upon a medium that a child just born will weigh 12 pounds, and in a solar year, if tolerably nursed, increased to 28 pounds.

I grant this food will be somewhat dear and therefore very proper for landlords, who, as they have already devoured most of the parents, seem to have the best title to the children.

Infant's flesh will be in season throughout the year, but more plentiful in March, and a little before and after; for we are told by a grave author, an eminent French physician, that fish being a prolific diet, there are more children born in Roman Catholic countries about nine months after Lent, the markets will be more glutted than usual, because the number of Popish infants, is at least three to one in this kingdom, and therefore it will have one other collateral advantage, by lessening the number of Papists among us.

I have already computed the charge of nursing a beggar's child (in which list I reckon all cottagers, laborers, and four-fifths of the farmers) to be about two shillings per annum, rags included; and I believe no gentleman would repine to give ten shillings for the carcass of a good fat child, which, as I have said, will make four dishes of excellent nutritive meat, when he hath only some particular friend, or his own family to dine with him. Thus the squire will learn to be a good landlord, and grow popular among his tenants, the mother will have eight shillings neat profit, and be fit for work till she produces another child.

Those who are more thrifty (as I must confess the times require) may flea the carcass; the skin of which, artificially dressed, will make admirable gloves for ladies, and summer boots for fine gentlemen.

As to our City of Dublin, shambles may be appointed for this purpose, in the most convenient parts of it, and butchers we may be assured will not be wanting; although I rather recommend buying the children alive, and dressing them hot from the knife, as we do roasting pigs.

A very worthy person, a true lover of his country, and whose virtues I highly esteem, was lately pleased, in discoursing on this matter, to offer a refinement upon my scheme. He said, that many gentlemen of this kingdom, having of late destroyed their deer, he conceived that the want of venison might be well supplied by the bodies of young lads and maidens, not exceeding fourteen years of age, nor under twelve; so great a number of both sexes in every country being now ready to starve for want of work and service: And these to be disposed of by their parents if alive, or otherwise by their nearest relations. But with due deference to so excellent a friend, and so deserving a patriot, I cannot be altogether in his sentiments; for as to the males, my American acquaintance assured me from frequent experience, that their flesh was generally tough and lean, like that of our school-boys, by continual exercise, and their taste disagreeable, and to fatten them would not answer the charge. Then as to the females, it would, I think, with humble submission, be a loss to the public, because they soon would become breeders themselves: And besides, it is not improbable that some scrupulous people might be apt to censure such a practice, (although indeed very unjustly) as a little bordering upon cruelty, which, I confess, hath always been with me the strongest objection against any project, how well so ever intended.

But in order to justify my friend, he confessed, that this expedient was put into his head by the famous Salmanaazor, a native of the island Formosa, who came from thence to London, above twenty years ago, and in conversation told my friend, that in his country, when any young person happened to be put to death, the executioner sold the carcass to persons of quality, as a prime dainty;

and that, in his time, the body of a plump girl of fifteen, who was crucified for an attempt to poison the Emperor, was sold to his imperial majesty's prime minister of state, and other great mandarins of the court in joints from the gibbet, at four hundred crowns. Neither indeed can I deny that if the same use were made of several plump young girls in this town, who without one single coin to their fortunes, cannot stir abroad without a chair, and appear at a playhouse and assemblies in foreign fineries which they never will pay for; the kingdom would not be the worse.

Some persons of a desponding spirit are in great concern about that vast number of poor people, who are aged, diseased, or maimed; and I have been desired to employ my thoughts what course may be taken, to ease the nation of so grievous an encumbrance. But I am not in the least pain upon that matter, because it is very well known, that they are everyday dying, and rotting, by cold and famine, and filth, and vermin, as fast as can be reasonably expected. And as to the young laborers, they are now in almost as hopeful a condition. They cannot get work, and consequently pine away from want of nourishment, to a degree, that if at any time they are accidentally hired to common labor, they have not strength to perform it, and thus the country and themselves are happily delivered from the evils to come.

I have too long digressed, and therefore shall return to my subject. I think the advantages by the proposal which I have made are obvious and many, as well as of the highest importance.

For first, as I have already observed, it would greatly lessen the number of Papists, with whom we are yearly over-run, being the principal breeders of the nation, as well as our most dangerous enemies, and who stay at home on purpose with a design to deliver the kingdom to the Pretender, hoping to take their advantage by the absence of so many good Protestants, who have chosen rather to leave their country, than stay at home and pay tithes against their conscience to an episcopal curate.

Secondly, the poorer tenants will have something valuable of their own, which by law may be made liable to a distress and help to pay their landlord's rent, their corn and cattle being already seized, and money a thing unknown.

Thirdly, whereas the maintenance of an hundred thousand children, from two years old, and upwards, cannot be computed at less than ten shillings a piece per annum, the nation's stock will be thereby increased fifty thousand pounds per annum, besides the profit of a new dish, introduced to the tables of all gentlemen of fortune in the kingdom, who have any refinement in taste. And the money will circulate among ourselves, the goods being entirely of our own growth and manufacture.

Fourthly, the constant breeders, besides the gain of eight shillings sterling per annum by the sale of their children, will be rid of the charge of maintaining them after the first year.

Fifthly, This food would likewise bring great custom to taverns, where the wine merchants will certainly be so prudent as to procure the best receipts for dressing it to perfection; and consequently have their houses frequented by all the fine gentlemen, who justly value themselves upon their knowledge in good eating; and a skilful cook, who understands how to oblige his guests, will contrive to make it as expensive as they please.

Sixthly, this would be a great inducement to marriage, which all wise nations have either encouraged by rewards, or enforced by laws and penalties. It would increase the care and tenderness of mothers towards their children, when they were sure of a settlement for life to the poor babes, provided in some sort by the public, to their annual profit instead of expense. We should soon see an honest emulation among the married women, which of them could bring the fattest child to the market. Men would become as fond of their wives, during the time of their pregnancy, as they are now of their mares in foal, their cows in calf, or sow when they are ready to give birth; nor offer to beat or kick them (as is too frequent a practice) for fear of a miscarriage.

Many other advantages might be enumerated. For instance, the addition of some thousand carcasses in our exportation of barreled beef: the propagation of swine's flesh, and improvement in the art of making good bacon, so much wanted among us by the great destruction of pigs, too frequent at our tables; which are no way comparable in taste or magnificence to a well grown, fat yearly child, which roasted whole will make a considerable figure at a Lord Mayor's feast, or any other public entertainment. But this, and many others, I omit, being studious of brevity.

Supposing that one thousand families in this city, would be constant customers for infants flesh, besides others who might have it at merry meetings, particularly at weddings and christenings, I compute that Dublin would take off annually about twenty thousand carcasses; and the rest of the kingdom (where probably they will be sold somewhat cheaper) the remaining eighty thousand.

I can think of no one objection, that will possibly be raised against this proposal, unless it should be urged, that the number of people will be thereby much lessened in the kingdom. This I freely own, and 'twas indeed one principal design in offering it to the world. I desire the reader will observe, that I calculate my remedy for this one individual Kingdom of Ireland, and for no other that ever was, is, or, I think, ever can be upon Earth. Therefore let no man talk to me of other expedients: Of taxing our absentees at five shillings a pound: Of using neither clothes, nor household furniture, except what is of our own growth and manufacture: Of utterly rejecting the materials and instruments that promote foreign luxury: Of curing the expensiveness of pride, vanity, idleness, and gaming in our women: Of introducing a vein of parsimony, prudence and temperance: Of learning to love our country, wherein we differ even from Laplanders, and the inhabitants of Topinamboo: Of quitting our animosities and factions, nor acting any longer like the Jews, who were murdering one another at the very moment their city was taken: Of being a little cautious not to sell our country and consciences for nothing: Of teaching landlords to have at least one degree of mercy towards their tenants. Lastly, of putting a spirit of honesty, industry, and skill into our shop-keepers, who, if a resolution could now be taken to buy only our native goods, would immediately unite to cheat and exact upon us in the price, the measure, and the goodness, nor could ever yet be brought to make one fair proposal of just dealing, though often and earnestly invited to it.

Therefore I repeat, let no man talk to me of these and the like expedients, 'till he hath at least some glimpse of hope, that there will ever be some hearty and sincere attempt to put them into practice.

But, as to myself, having been wearied out for many years with offering vain, idle, visionary thoughts, and at length utterly despairing of success, I fortunately fell upon this proposal, which, as it is wholly new, so it hath something solid and real, of no expense and little trouble, full in our own power, and whereby we can incur no danger in disobliging England. For this kind of commodity will not bear exportation, and flesh being of too tender a consistence, to admit a long continuance in salt, although perhaps I could name a country, which would be glad to eat up our whole nation without it.

After all, I am not so violently bent upon my own opinion, as to reject any offer, proposed by wise men, which shall be found equally innocent, cheap, easy, and effectual. But before something of that kind shall be advanced in contradiction to my scheme, and offering a better, I desire the author or authors will be pleased maturely to consider two points. First, as things now stand, how they will be able to find food and raiment for a hundred thousand useless mouths and backs. And secondly, There being a round million of creatures in humane figure throughout this kingdom, whose whole subsistence put into a common stock, would leave them in debt two million of pounds sterling, adding those who are beggars by profession, to the bulk of farmers, cottagers and laborers, with their wives and children, who are beggars in effect; I desire those politicians who dislike my overture, and may perhaps be so bold to attempt an answer, that they will first ask the parents of these mortals, whether they would not at this day think it a great happiness to have been sold for food at a year old, in the manner I prescribe, and thereby have avoided such a perpetual scene of misfortunes, as they have since gone through, by the oppression of landlords, the impossibility of paying rent without money or trade, the want of common sustenance, with neither house nor clothes to cover them from the merciless weather, and the most inevitable prospect of requiring similar, or greater miseries, upon their breed forever.

I profess, in the sincerity of my heart, that I have not the least personal interest in endeavoring to promote this necessary work, having no other motive than the public good of my country, by advancing our trade, providing for infants, relieving the poor, and giving some pleasure to the rich. I have no children, by which I can propose to get a single penny; the youngest being nine years old, and my wife past child-bearing.

*"Yet, through despair, of God and man accurst,
He lost his bishopric, and hang'd or burst."*

JUDAS

Jonathan Swift

1731

By the just vengeance of incensed skies,
Poor Bishop Judas late repenting dies.
The Jews engaged him with a paltry bribe,
Amounting hardly to a crown a-tribe;
Which though his conscience forced him to restore,
(And parsons tell us, no man can do more,)
Yet, through despair, of God and man accurst,
He lost his bishopric, and hang'd or burst.
Those former ages differ'd much from this;
Judas betray'd his master with a kiss:
But some have kiss'd the gospel fifty times,
Whose perjury's the least of all their crimes;
Some who can perjure through a two inch-board,
Yet keep their bishoprics, and 'scape the cord:
Like hemp, which, by a skilful spinster drawn
To slender threads, may sometimes pass for lawn.
As ancient Judas by transgression fell,
And burst asunder ere he went to hell;
So could we see a set of new Iscariots
Come headlong tumbling from their mitred chariots;
Each modern Judas perish like the first,
Drop from the tree with all his bowels burst;
Who could forbear, that view'd each guilty face,
To cry, "Lo! Judas gone to his own place,
His habitation let all men forsake,
And let his bishopric another take!"

"… those that cannot or dare not make war in person employ others to do it for them."

A Digression on the Nature, Usefulness, and Necessity of Wars and Quarrels

Taken from *A Tale of a Tub and Other Works*

Jonathan Swift

1889

This being a matter of great consequence, the author intends to treat it methodically and at large in a treatise apart, and here to give only some hints of what his large treatise contains. The state of war, natural to all creatures. War is an attempt to take by violence from others a part of what they have and we want. Every man, fully sensible of his own merit, and finding it not duly regarded by others, has a natural right to take from them all that he thinks due to himself; and every creature, finding its own wants more than those of others, has the same right to take everything its nature requires. Brutes, much more modest in their pretensions this way than men, and mean men more than great ones. The higher one raises his pretensions this way, the more bustle he makes about them, and the more success he has, the greater hero. Thus greater souls, in proportion to their superior merit, claim a greater right to take everything from meaner folks. This the true foundation of grandeur and heroism, and of the distinction of degrees among men. War, therefore, necessary to establish subordination, and to found cities, kingdoms, &c., as also to purge bodies politic of gross humours. Wise princes find it necessary to have wars abroad to keep peace at home. War, famine, and pestilence, the usual cures for corruption in bodies politic. A comparison of these three - the author is to write a panegyric on each of them. The greatest part of mankind loves war more than peace. They are but few and mean-spirited that live in peace with all men. The modest and meek of all kinds always a prey to those of more noble or stronger appetites. The inclination to war universal; those that cannot or dare not make war in person employ others to do it for them. This maintains bullies, bravoes, cut-throats, lawyers, soldiers, &c. Most professions would be useless if all were peaceable. Hence brutes want neither smiths nor lawyers, magistrates nor joiners, soldiers or surgeons. Brutes having but narrow appetites, are incapable of carrying on or perpetuating war against their own species, or of being led out in troops and multitudes to destroy one another. These prerogatives proper to man alone. The excellency of human nature demonstrated by the vast train of appetites, passions, wants, &c., that attend it. This matter to be more fully treated in the author's panegyric on mankind.

"Chimnies with Scorn rejecting Smoak,..."

To Quilca, a Country House not in Good Repair

Jonathan Swift

1725

Let me thy Properties explain,

A rotten Cabin, dropping Rain;

Chimnies with Scorn rejecting Smoak;

Stools, Tables, Chairs, and Bed-steds broke:

Here Elements have lost their Vses,

Air ripens not, nor Earth produces:

In vain we make poor Sheelah toil,

Fire will not roast, nor Water boil.

Thro' all the Vallies, Hills, and Plains,

The Goddess Want in Triumph reigns;

And her chief Officers of State,

Sloth, Dirt, and Theft around her wait.

"What is a man but a topsy-turvy creature, his animal faculties perpetually mounted on his rational."

A Meditation Upon a Broomstick

According to the Style and Manner of the Hon. Robert Boyle's Meditations.

Jonathan Swift

1704

This single stick, which you now behold ingloriously lying in that neglected corner, I once knew in a flourishing state in a forest. It was full of sap, full of leaves, and full of boughs; but now in vain does the busy art of man pretend to vie with nature, by tying that withered bundle of twigs to its sapless trunk; it is now at best but the reverse of what it was, a tree turned upside-down, the branches on the earth, and the root in the air; it is now handled by every dirty wench, condemned to do her drudgery, and, by a capricious kind of fate, destined to make other things clean, and be nasty itself; at length, worn to the stumps in the service of the maids, it is either thrown out of doors or condemned to the last use—of kindling a fire. When I behold this I sighed, and said within myself, "Surely mortal man is a broomstick!" Nature sent him into the world strong and lusty, in a thriving condition, wearing his own hair on his head, the proper branches of this reasoning vegetable, till the axe of intemperance has lopped off his green boughs, and left him a withered trunk; he then flies to art, and puts on a periwig, valuing himself upon an unnatural bundle of hairs, all covered with powder, that never grew on his head; but now should this our broomstick pretend to enter the scene, proud of those birchen spoils it never bore, and all covered with dust, through the sweepings of the finest lady's chamber, we should be apt to ridicule and despise its vanity. Partial judges that we are of our own excellencies, and other men's defaults!

But a broomstick, perhaps you will say, is an emblem of a tree standing on its head; and pray what is a man but a topsy-turvy creature, his animal faculties perpetually mounted on his rational, his head where his heels should be, grovelling on the earth? And yet, with all his faults, he sets up to be a universal reformer and corrector of abuses, a remover of grievances, rakes into every slut's corner of nature, bringing hidden corruptions to the light, and raises a mighty dust where there was none before, sharing deeply all the while in the very same pollutions he pretends to sweep away. His last days are spent in slavery to women, and generally the least deserving; till, worn to the stumps, like his brother besom, he is either kicked out of doors, or made use of to kindle flames for others to warm themselves by.

*"Every man desires to live long;
but no man would be old."*

Thoughts on Various Subjects

Jonathan Swift

1708

- We have just enough religion to make us hate, but not enough to make us love one another.

- Reflect on things past as wars, negotiations, factions, etc. We enter so little into those interests, that we wonder how men could possibly be so busy and concerned for things so transitory; look on the present times, we find the same humour, yet wonder not at all.

- A wise man endeavours, by considering all circumstances, to make conjectures and form conclusions; but the smallest accident intervening (and in the course of affairs it is impossible to foresee all) does often produce such turns and changes, that at last he is just as much in doubt of events as the most ignorant and inexperienced person.

- Positiveness is a good quality for preachers and orators, because he that would obtrude his thoughts and reasons upon a multitude, will convince others the more, as he appears convinced himself.

- How is it possible to expect that mankind will take advice, when they will not so much as take warning?

- I forget whether Advice be among the lost things which Aristo says are to be found in the moon; that and Time ought to have been there.

- No preacher is listened to but Time, which gives us the same train and turn of thought that older people have tried in vain to put into our heads before.

- When we desire or solicit anything, our minds run wholly on the good side or circumstances of it; when it is obtained, our minds run wholly on the bad ones.

- In a glass-house the workmen often fling in a small quantity of fresh coals, which seems to disturb the fire, but very much enlivens it. This seems to allude to a gentle stirring of the passions, that the mind may not languish.

- Religion seems to have grown an infant with age, and requires miracles to nurse it, as it had in its infancy.

- All fits of pleasure are balanced by an equal degree of pain or languor; it is like spending this year part of the next year's revenue.

- The latter part of a wise man's life is taken up in curing the follies, prejudices, and false opinions he had contracted in the former.

- Would a writer know how to behave himself with relation to posterity, let him consider in old books what he finds that he is glad to know, and what omissions he most laments.

- Whatever the poets pretend, it is plain they give immortality to none but themselves; it is Homer and Virgil we reverence and admire, not Achilles or Æneas. With historians it is quite the contrary; our thoughts are taken up with the actions, persons, and events we read, and we little regard the authors.

- When a true genius appears in the world you may know him by this sign; that the dunces are all in confederacy against him.

- Men who possess all the advantages of life, are in a state where there are many accidents to disorder and discompose, but few to please them.

- It is unwise to punish cowards with ignominy, for if they had regarded that they would not have been cowards; death is their proper punishment, because they fear it most.

- The greatest inventions were produced in the times of ignorance, as the use of the compass, gunpowder, and printing, and by the dullest nation, as the Germans.

- One argument to prove that the common relations of ghosts and spectres are generally false, may be drawn from the opinion held that spirits are never seen by more than one person at a time; that is to say, it seldom happens to above one person in a company to be possessed with any high degree of spleen or melancholy.

- I am apt to think that, in the day of Judgment, there will be small allowance given to the wise for their want of morals, nor to the ignorant for their want of faith, because both are without excuse. This renders the advantages equal of ignorance and knowledge. But, some scruples in the wise, and some vices in the ignorant, will perhaps be forgiven upon the strength of temptation to each.

- The value of several circumstances in story lessens very much by distance of time, though some minute circumstances are very valuable; and it requires great judgment in a writer to distinguish.

- It is grown a word of course for writers to say, "This critical age," as divines say, "This sinful age."

➢ It is pleasant to observe how free the present age is in laying taxes on the next. Future ages shall talk of this; this shall be famous to all posterity. Whereas their time and thoughts will be taken up about present things, as ours are now.

➢ The chameleon, who is said to feed upon nothing but air, hath, of all animals, the nimblest tongue.

➢ When a man is made a spiritual peer he loses his surname; when a temporal, his Christian name.

➢ It is in disputes as in armies, where the weaker side sets up false lights, and makes a great noise, to make the enemy believe them more numerous and strong than they really are.

➢ Some men, under the notions of weeding out prejudices, eradicate virtue, honesty, and religion.

➢ In all well-instituted commonwealths, care has been taken to limit men's possessions; which is done for many reasons, and among the rest, for one which perhaps is not often considered: that when bounds are set to men's desires, after they have acquired as much as the laws will permit them, their private interest is at an end, and they have nothing to do but to take care of the public.

➢ There are but three ways for a man to revenge himself of the censure of the world: to despise it, to return the like, or to endeavour to live so as to avoid it. The first of these is usually pretended, the last is almost impossible; the universal practice is for the second.

➢ I never heard a finer piece of satire against lawyers than that of astrologers, when they pretend by rules of art to tell when a suit will end, and whether to the advantage of the plaintiff or defendant; thus making the matter depend entirely upon the influence of the stars, without the least regard to the merits of the cause.

➢ The expression in Apocrypha about Tobit and his dog following him I have often heard ridiculed, yet Homer has the same words of Telemachus more than once; and Virgil says something like it of Evander. And I take the book of Tobit to be partly poetical.

- I have known some men possessed of good qualities, which were very serviceable to others, but useless to themselves; like a sundial on the front of a house, to inform the neighbours and passengers, but not the owner within.

- If a man would register all his opinions upon love, politics, religion, learning, etc., beginning from his youth and so go on to old age, what a bundle of inconsistencies and contradictions would appear at last!

- What they do in heaven we are ignorant of; what they do not we are told expressly: that they neither marry, nor are given in marriage.

- It is a miserable thing to live in suspense; it is the life of a spider.

- The Stoical scheme of supplying our wants by lopping off our desires, is like cutting off our feet when we want shoes.

- Physicians ought not to give their judgment of religion, for the same reason that butchers are not admitted to be jurors upon life and death.

- The reason why so few marriages are happy, is, because young ladies spend their time in making nets, not in making cages.

- If a man will observe as he walks the streets, I believe he will find the merriest countenances in mourning coaches.

- Nothing more unqualifies a man to act with prudence than a misfortune that is attended with shame and guilt.

- The power of fortune is confessed only by the miserable; for the happy impute all their success to prudence or merit.

- Ambition often puts men upon doing the meanest offices; so climbing is performed in the same posture with creeping.

- Censure is the tax a man pays to the public for being eminent.

- Although men are accused for not knowing their own weakness, yet perhaps as few know their own strength. It is, in men as in soils, where sometimes there is a vein of gold which the owner knows not of.

- Satire is reckoned the easiest of all wit, but I take it to be otherwise in very bad times: for it is as hard to satirise well a man of distinguished vices, as to praise well a man of distinguished virtues. It is easy enough to do either to people of moderate characters.

- Invention is the talent of youth, and judgment of age; so that our judgment grows harder to please, when we have fewer things to offer it: this goes through the whole commerce of life. When we are old, our friends find it difficult to please us, and are less concerned whether we be pleased or no.

- No wise man ever wished to be younger.

- An idle reason lessens the weight of the good ones you gave before.

- The motives of the best actions will not bear too strict an inquiry. It is allowed that the cause of most actions, good or bad, may be resolved into the love of ourselves; but the self-love of some men inclines them to please others, and the self-love of others is wholly employed in pleasing themselves. This makes the great distinction between virtue and vice. Religion is the best motive of all actions, yet religion is allowed to be the highest instance of self-love.

- Old men view best at a distance with the eyes of their understanding as well as with those of nature.

- Some people take more care to hide their wisdom than their folly.

- Anthony Henley's farmer, dying of an asthma, said, "Well, if I can get this breath once out, I'll take care it never got in again."

- The humour of exploding many things under the name of trifles, fopperies, and only imaginary goods, is a very false proof either of wisdom or magnanimity, and a great check to virtuous actions. For instance, with regard to fame, there is in most people a reluctance and unwillingness to be forgotten. We observe, even among the vulgar, how fond they are to have an inscription over their grave. It requires but little philosophy to discover and observe that there is no intrinsic value in all this; however, if it be founded in our nature as an incitement to virtue, it ought not to be ridiculed.

- Complaint is the largest tribute heaven receives, and the sincerest part of our devotion.

- The common fluency of speech in many men, and most women, is owing to a scarcity of matter, and a scarcity of words; for whoever is a master of language, and hath a mind full of ideas, will be apt, in speaking, to hesitate upon the choice of both; whereas common speakers have only one set of ideas, and one set of words to clothe them in, and these are always ready at the mouth. So people come faster out of a church when it is almost empty, than when a crowd is at the door.

- Few are qualified to shine in company; but it is in most men's power to be agreeable. The reason, therefore, why conversation runs so low at present, is not the defect of understanding, but pride, vanity, ill-nature, affectation, singularity, positiveness, or some other vice, the effect of a wrong education.

- To be vain is rather a mark of humility than pride. Vain men delight in telling what honours have been done them, what great company they have kept, and the like, by which they plainly confess that these honours were more than their due, and such as their friends would not believe if they had not been told: whereas a man truly proud thinks the greatest honours below his merit, and consequently scorns to boast. I therefore deliver it as a maxim, that whoever desires the character of a proud man, ought to conceal his vanity.

- Law, in a free country, is, or ought to be, the determination of the majority of those who have property in land.

- One argument used to the disadvantage of Providence I take to be a very strong one in its defence. It is objected that storms and tempests, unfruitful seasons, serpents, spiders, flies, and other noxious or troublesome animals, with many more instances of the like kind, discover an imperfection in nature, because human life would be much easier without them; but the design of Providence may clearly be perceived in this proceeding. The motions of the sun and moon—in short, the whole system of the universe, as far as philosophers have been able to discover and observe, are in the utmost degree of regularity and perfection; but wherever God hath left to man the power of interposing a remedy by thought or labour, there he hath placed things in a state of imperfection, on purpose to stir up human industry, without which life would stagnate, or, indeed, rather, could not subsist at all: Curis accuunt mortalia corda.

- Praise is the daughter of present power.

- How inconsistent is man with himself!

- I have known several persons of great fame for wisdom in public affairs and counsels governed by foolish servants.

- I have known great Ministers, distinguished for wit and learning, who preferred none but dunces.

- I have known men of great valour cowards to their wives.

- I have known men of the greatest cunning perpetually cheated.

- I knew three great Ministers, who could exactly compute and settle the accounts of a kingdom, but were wholly ignorant of their own economy.

- The preaching of divines helps to preserve well-inclined men in the course of virtue, but seldom or never reclaims the vicious.

- Princes usually make wiser choices than the servants whom they trust for the disposal of places: I have known a prince, more than once, choose an able Minister, but I never observed that Minister to use his credit in the disposal of an employment to a person whom he thought the fittest for it. One of the greatest in this age owned and excused the matter from the violence of parties and the unreasonableness of friends.

➢ Small causes are sufficient to make a man uneasy when great ones are not in the way. For want of a block he will stumble at a straw.

➢ Dignity, high station, or great riches, are in some sort necessary to old men, in order to keep the younger at a distance, who are otherwise too apt to insult them upon the score of their age.

➢ Every man desires to live long; but no man would be old.

➢ Love of flattery in most men proceeds from the mean opinion they have of themselves; in women from the contrary.

➢ If books and laws continue to increase as they have done for fifty years past, I am in some concern for future ages how any man will be learned, or any man a lawyer.

➢ Kings are commonly said to have long hands; I wish they had as long ears.

➢ Princes in their infancy, childhood, and youth are said to discover prodigious parts and wit, to speak things that surprise and astonish. Strange, so many hopeful princes, and so many shameful kings! If they happen to die young, they would have been prodigies of wisdom and virtue. If they live, they are often prodigies indeed, but of another sort.

➢ Politics, as the word is commonly understood, are nothing but corruptions, and consequently of no use to a good king or a good ministry; for which reason Courts are so overrun with politics.

➢ A nice man is a man of nasty ideas.

➢ Apollo was held the god of physic and sender of diseases. Both were originally the same trade, and still continue.

➢ Old men and comets have been reverenced for the same reason: their long beards, and pretences to foretell events.

➢ A person was asked at court, what he thought of an ambassador and his train, who were all embroidery and lace, full of bows, cringes, and gestures; he said, it was Solomon's importation, gold and apes.

➢ Most sorts of diversion in men, children, and other animals, is an imitation of fighting.

➢ Augustus meeting an ass with a lucky name foretold himself good fortune. I meet many asses, but none of them have lucky names.

➢ If a man makes me keep my distance, the comfort is he keeps his at the same time.

➢ Who can deny that all men are violent lovers of truth when we see them so positive in their errors, which they will maintain out of their zeal to truth, although they contradict themselves every day of their lives?

➢ That was excellently observed, say I, when I read a passage in an author, where his opinion agrees with mine. When we differ, there I pronounce him to be mistaken.

➢ Very few men, properly speaking, live at present, but are providing to live another time.

➢ Laws penned with the utmost care and exactness, and in the vulgar language, are often perverted to wrong meanings; then why should we wonder that the Bible is so?

➢ Although men are accused for not knowing their weakness, yet perhaps as few know their own strength.

➢ A man seeing a wasp creeping into a vial filled with honey, that was hung on a fruit tree, said thus: "Why, thou sottish animal, art thou mad to go into that vial, where you see many hundred of your kind there dying in it before you?" "The reproach is just," answered the wasp, "but not from you men, who are so far from taking example by other people's follies, that you will not take warning by your own. If after falling several times into this vial, and escaping by chance, I should fall in again, I should then but resemble you."

- An old miser kept a tame jackdaw, that used to steal pieces of money, and hide them in a hole, which the cat observing, asked why he would hoard up those round shining things that he could make no use of? "Why," said the jackdaw, "my master has a whole chest full, and makes no more use of them than I."

- Men are content to be laughed at for their wit, but not for their folly.

- If the men of wit and genius would resolve never to complain in their works of critics and detractors, the next age would not know that they ever had any.

- After all the maxims and systems of trade and commerce, a stander-by would think the affairs of the world were most ridiculously contrived.

- There are few countries which, if well cultivated, would not support double the number of their inhabitants, and yet fewer where one-third of the people are not extremely stinted even in the necessaries of life. I send out twenty barrels of corn, which would maintain a family in bread for a year, and I bring back in return a vessel of wine, which half a dozen good follows would drink in less than a month, at the expense of their health and reason.

- A man would have but few spectators, if he offered to show for threepence how he could thrust a red-hot iron into a barrel of gunpowder, and it should not take fire.

*"And that's the reason, some folks think,
He left behind so great a stink."*

A Satirical Elegy

On the Death of a Late Famous General

by Jonathan Swift

1722

His Grace! impossible! what, dead!

Of old age too, and in his bed!

And could that mighty warrior fall,

And so inglorious, after all?

Well, since he's gone, no matter how,

The last loud trump must wake him now;

And, trust me, as the noise grows stronger,

He'd wish to sleep a little longer.

And could he be indeed so old

As by the newspapers we're told?

Threescore, I think, is pretty high;

'Twas time in conscience he should die!

This world he cumber'd long enough;

He burnt his candle to the snuff;

And that's the reason, some folks think,

He left behind so great a stink.

Behold his funeral appears,

Nor widows' sighs, nor orphans' tears,

Wont at such times each heart to pierce,

Attend the progress of his hearse.

But what of that? his friends may say,

He had those honours in his day.

True to his profit and his pride,

He made them weep before he died.

Come hither, all ye empty things!

Ye bubbles rais'd by breath of kings!

Who float upon the tide of state;

A MODEST PROPOSAL / A MODERN PROPOSAL

Come hither, and behold your fate!

Let pride be taught by this rebuke,

How very mean a thing's a duke;

From all his ill-got honours flung,

Turn'd to that dirt from whence he sprung.

"If Christianity were once abolished, how could the Freethinkers, the strong reasoners, and the men of profound learning be able to find another subject so calculated in all points whereon to display their abilities?"

An Argument Against Abolishing Christianity

An argument to prove that the abolishing of Christianity in England may, as things now stand, be attended with some inconveniences, and perhaps not produce those many good effects proposed thereby.

by Jonathan Swift

1708

I AM very sensible what a weakness and presumption it is to reason against the general humor and disposition of the world. I remember it was with great justice, and a due regard to the freedom, both of the public and the press, forbidden upon several penalties to write, or discourse, or lay wagers against the — even before it was confirmed by Parliament; because that was looked upon as a design to oppose the current of the people, which, besides the folly of it, is a manifest breach of the fundamental law, that makes this majority of opinions the voice of God. In like manner, and for the very same reasons, it may perhaps be neither safe nor prudent to argue against the abolishing of Christianity, at a juncture when all parties seem so unanimously determined upon the point, as we cannot but allow from their actions, their discourses, and their writings. However, I know not how, whether from the affectation of singularity, or the perverseness of human nature, but so it unhappily falls out, that I cannot be entirely of this opinion. Nay, though I were sure an order were issued for my immediate prosecution by the Attorney-General, I should still confess, that in the present posture of our affairs at home or abroad, I do not yet see the absolute necessity of extirpating the Christian religion from among us.

This perhaps may appear too great a paradox even for our wise and parodoxical age to endure; therefore I shall handle it with all tenderness and with the utmost deference to that great and profound majority which is of another sentiment.

And yet the curious may please to observe, how much the genius of a nation is liable to alter in half an age. I have heard it affirmed for certain by some very odd people, that the contrary opinion was even in their memories as much in vogue as the other is now; and that a project for the abolishing of Christianity would then have appeared as singular, and been thought as absurd, as it would be at this time to write or discourse in its defense.

Therefore I freely own, that all appearances are against me. The system of the Gospel, after the fate of other systems, is generally antiquated and exploded, and the mass or body of the common people, among whom it seems to have had its latest credit, are now grown as much ashamed of it as their betters; opinions, like fashions, always descending from those of quality to the middle sort, and thence to the vulgar, where at length they are dropped and vanish.

But here I would not be mistaken, and must therefore be so bold as to borrow a distinction from the writers on the other side, when they make a difference betwixt nominal and real Trinitarians. I hope no reader imagines me so weak to stand up in the defense of real Christianity, such as used in primitive times (if we may believe the authors of those ages) to have an influence upon men's belief and actions. To offer at the restoring of that, would indeed be a wild project: it would be to dig up foundations; to destroy at one blow all the wit, and half the learning of the kingdom; to break the entire frame and constitution of things; to ruin trade, extinguish arts and sciences, with the professors of them; in short, to turn our courts, exchanges, and shops into deserts; and would be full as absurd as the proposal of Horace, where he advises the Romans, all in a body, to leave their city, and seek a new seat in some remote part of the world, by way of a cure for the corruption of their manners.

Therefore I think this caution was in itself altogether unnecessary (which I have inserted only to prevent all possibility of caviling), since every candid reader will easily understand my discourse to be intended only in defense of nominal Christianity, the other having been for some time wholly laid aside by general consent, as utterly inconsistent with all our present schemes of wealth and power.

But why we should therefore cut off the name and title of Christians, although the general opinion and resolution be so violent for it, I confess I cannot (with submission) apprehend the consequence necessary. However, since the undertakers propose such wonderful advantages to the nation by this project, and advance many plausible objections against the system of Christianity, I shall briefly consider the strength of both, fairly allow them their greatest weight, and offer such answers as I think most reasonable. After which I will beg leave to show what inconveniences may possibly happen by such an innovation, in the present posture of our affairs.

First, one great advantage proposed by the abolishing of Christianity is, that it would very much enlarge and establish liberty of conscience, that great bulwark of our nation, and of the Protestant religion, which is still too much limited by priestcraft, notwithstanding all the good intentions of the legislature, as we have lately found by a severe instance. For it is confidently reported, that two young gentlemen of real hopes, bright wit, and profound judgment, who, upon a thorough examination of causes and effects, and by the mere force of natural abilities, without the least tincture of learning, having made a discovery that there was no God, and generously communicating their thoughts for the good of the public, were some time ago, by an unparalleled severity, and upon I know not what obsolete law, broke for blasphemy. And as it has been wisely observed, if persecution once begins, no man alive knows how far it may reach, or where it will end.

In answer to all which, with deference to wiser judgments, I think this rather shows the necessity of a nominal religion among us. Great wits love to be free with the highest objects; and if they cannot be allowed a god to revile or renounce, they will speak evil of dignities, abuse the government, and reflect upon the ministry, which I am sure few will deny to be of much more pernicious consequence, according to the saying of Tiberius, DEORUM OFFENSA DIIS CUROE. As to the particular fact related, I think it is not fair to argue from one instance, perhaps another cannot be produced: yet (to the comfort of all those who may be apprehensive of persecution) blasphemy we know is freely spoke a million of times in every coffee-house and tavern, or wherever else good company meet. It must be allowed, indeed, that to break an English free-born officer only for blasphemy was, to speak the gentlest of such an action, a very high strain of absolute power. Little can be said in excuse for the general; perhaps he was afraid it might give offence to the allies, among whom, for aught we know, it may be the custom of the country to believe a God. But if he argued, as some have done, upon a mistaken principle, that an officer who is guilty of speaking blasphemy may, some time or other, proceed so far as to raise a mutiny, the consequence is by no means to be admitted: for surely the commander of an English army is like to be but ill obeyed whose soldiers fear and reverence him as little as they do a Deity.

It is further objected against the Gospel system that it obliges men to the belief of things too difficult for Freethinkers, and such who have shook off the prejudices that usually cling to a confined education. To which I answer, that men should be cautious how they raise objections which reflect upon the wisdom of the nation. Is not everybody freely allowed to believe whatever he pleases, and to publish his belief to the world whenever he thinks fit, especially if it serves to strengthen the party which is in the right? Would any indifferent foreigner, who should read the trumpery lately written by Asgil, Tindal, Toland, Coward, and forty more, imagine the Gospel to be our rule of faith, and to be confirmed by Parliaments? Does any man either believe, or say he believes, or desire to have it thought that he says he believes, one syllable of the matter? And is any man worse received upon that score, or does he find his want of nominal faith a disadvantage to him in the pursuit of any civil or military employment? What if there be an old dormant statute or two against him, are they not now obsolete, to a degree, that Empson and Dudley themselves, if they were now alive, would find it impossible to put them in execution?

It is likewise urged, that there are, by computation, in this kingdom, above ten thousand parsons, whose revenues, added to those of my lords the bishops, would suffice to maintain at least two hundred young gentlemen of wit and pleasure, and free-thinking, enemies to priestcraft, narrow principles, pedantry, and prejudices, who might be an ornament to the court and town: and then again, so a great number of able [bodied] divines might be a recruit to our fleet and armies. This indeed appears to be a consideration of some weight; but then, on the other side, several things deserve to be considered likewise: as, first, whether it may not be thought necessary that in certain tracts of country, like what we call parishes, there should be one man at least of abilities to read and write. Then it seems a wrong computation that the revenues of the Church throughout this island would be large enough to maintain two hundred young gentlemen, or even half that number, after the present refined way of living, that is, to allow each of them such a rent as, in the modern form of speech, would make them easy. But still there is in this project a greater mischief behind; and we ought to beware of the woman's folly, who killed the hen that every morning laid her a golden egg. For, pray what would become of the race of men in the next age, if we had nothing to trust to beside the scrofulous consumptive production furnished by our men of wit and pleasure, when, having squandered away their vigor, health, and estates, they are forced, by some disagreeable marriage, to piece up their broken fortunes, and entail rottenness and politeness on their posterity? Now, here are ten thousand persons reduced, by the wise regulations of Henry VIII., to the necessity of a low diet, and moderate exercise, who are the only great restorers of our breed, without which the nation would in an age or two become one great hospital.

Another advantage proposed by the abolishing of Christianity is the clear gain of one day in seven, which is now entirely lost, and consequently the kingdom one seventh less considerable in trade, business, and pleasure; besides the loss to the public of so many stately structures now in the hands of the clergy, which might be converted into play-houses, exchanges, market-houses, common dormitories, and other public edifices.

I hope I shall be forgiven a hard word if I call this a perfect cavil. I readily own there hath been an old custom, time out of mind, for people to assemble in the churches every Sunday, and that shops are still frequently shut, in order, as it is conceived, to preserve the memory of that ancient practice; but how this can prove a hindrance to business or pleasure is hard to imagine. What if the men of pleasure are forced, one day in the week, to game at home instead of the chocolate-house? Are not the taverns and coffee-houses open? Can there be a more convenient season for taking a dose of physic? Is not that the chief day for traders to sum up the accounts of the week, and for lawyers to prepare their briefs? But I would fain know how it can be pretended that the churches are misapplied? Where are more appointments and rendezvous of gallantry? Where more care to appear in the foremost box, with greater advantage of dress? Where more meetings for business? Where more bargains driven of all sorts? And where so many conveniences or incitements to sleep?

There is one advantage greater than any of the foregoing, proposed by the abolishing of Christianity, that it will utterly extinguish parties among us, by removing those factious distinctions of high and low church, of Whig and Tory, Presbyterian and Church of England, which are now so many mutual clogs upon public proceedings, and are apt to prefer the gratifying themselves or depressing their adversaries before the most important interest of the State.

I confess, if it were certain that so great an advantage would redound to the nation by this expedient, I would submit, and be silent; but will any man say, that if the words, whoring, drinking, cheating, lying, stealing, were, by Act of Parliament, ejected out of the English tongue and dictionaries, we should all awake next morning chaste and temperate, honest and just, and lovers of truth? Is this a fair consequence? Or if the physicians would forbid us to pronounce the words pox, gout, rheumatism, and stone, would that expedient serve like so many talisman to destroy the diseases themselves? Are party and faction rooted in men's hearts no deeper than phrases borrowed from religion, or founded upon no firmer principles? And is our language so poor that we cannot find other terms to express them? Are envy, pride, avarice, and ambition such ill nomenclatures, that they cannot furnish appellations for their owners? Will not heydukes and mamalukes, mandarins and patshaws, or any other words formed at pleasure, serve to distinguish those who are in the ministry from others who would be in it if they could? What, for instance, is easier than to vary the form of speech, and instead of the word church, make it a question in politics, whether the monument be in danger? Because religion was nearest at hand to furnish a few convenient phrases, is our invention so barren we can find no other? Suppose, for argument sake, that the Tories favoured Margarita, the Whigs, Mrs. Tofts, and the Trimmers, Valentini, would not Margaritians, Toftians, and Valentinians be very tolerable marks of distinction? The Prasini and Veniti, two most virulent factions in Italy, began, if I remember right, by a distinction of colors in ribbons, which we might do with as good a grace about the dignity of the blue and the green, and serve as properly to divide the Court, the Parliament, and the kingdom between them, as any terms of art whatsoever, borrowed from religion. And therefore I think there is little force in this objection against Christianity, or prospect of so great an advantage as is proposed in the abolishing of it.

It is again objected, as a very absurd, ridiculous custom, that a set of men should be suffered, much less employed and hired, to bawl one day in seven against the lawfulness of those methods most in use towards the pursuit of greatness, riches, and pleasure, which are the constant practice of all men alive on the other six. But this objection is, I think, a little unworthy so refined an age as ours. Let us argue this matter calmly. I appeal to the breast of any polite Free-thinker, whether, in the pursuit of gratifying a pre-dominant passion, he hath not always felt a wonderful incitement, by reflecting it was a thing forbidden; and therefore we see, in order to cultivate this test, the wisdom of the nation hath taken special care that the ladies should be furnished with prohibited silks, and the men with prohibited wine. And indeed it were to be wished that some other prohibitions were promoted, in order to improve the pleasures of the town, which, for want of such expedients, begin already, as I am told, to flag and grow languid, giving way daily to cruel inroads from the spleen.

'Tis likewise proposed, as a great advantage to the public, that if we once discard the system of the Gospel, all religion will of course be banished for ever, and consequently along with it those grievous prejudices of education which, under the names of conscience, honor, justice, and the like, are so apt to disturb the peace of human minds, and the notions whereof are so hard to be eradicated by right reason or free-thinking, sometimes during the whole course of our lives.

Here first I observe how difficult it is to get rid of a phrase which the world has once grown fond of, though the occasion that first produced it be entirely taken away. For some years past, if a man had but an ill-favoured nose, the deep thinkers of the age would, some way or other contrive to impute the cause to the prejudice of his education. From this fountain were said to be derived all our foolish notions of justice, piety, love of our country; all our opinions of God or a future state, heaven, hell, and the like; and there might formerly perhaps have been some pretence for this charge. But so effectual care hath been since taken to remove those prejudices, by an entire change in the methods of education, that (with honor I mention it to our polite innovators) the young gentlemen, who are now on the scene, seem to have not the least tincture left of those infusions, or string of those weeds, and by consequence the reason for abolishing nominal Christianity upon that pretext is wholly ceased.

For the rest, it may perhaps admit a controversy, whether the banishing all notions of religion whatsoever would be inconvenient for the vulgar. Not that I am in the least of opinion with those who hold religion to have been the invention of politicians, to keep the lower part of the world in awe by the fear of invisible powers; unless mankind were then very different from what it is now; for I look upon the mass or body of our people here in England to be as Freethinkers, that is to say, as staunch unbelievers, as any of the highest rank. But I conceive some scattered notions about a superior power to be of singular use for the common people, as furnishing excellent materials to keep children quiet when they grow peevish, and providing topics of amusement in a tedious winter night.

Lastly, it is proposed, as a singular advantage, that the abolishing of Christianity will very much contribute to the uniting of Protestants, by enlarging the terms of communion, so as to take in all sorts of Dissenters, who are now shut out of the pale upon account of a few ceremonies, which all sides confess to be things indifferent. That this alone will effectually answer the great ends of a scheme for comprehension, by opening a large noble gate, at which all bodies may enter; whereas the chaffering with Dissenters, and dodging about this or t'other ceremony, is but like opening a few wickets, and leaving them at jar, by which no more than one can get in at a time, and that not without stooping, and sideling, and squeezing his body.

To all this I answer, that there is one darling inclination of mankind which usually affects to be a retainer to religion, though she be neither its parent, its godmother, nor its friend. I mean the spirit of opposition, that lived long before Christianity, and can easily subsist without it. Let us, for instance, examine wherein the opposition of sectaries among us consists. We shall find Christianity to have no share in it at all. Does the Gospel anywhere prescribe a starched, squeezed countenance, a stiff formal gait, a singularity of manners and habit, or any affected forms and modes of speech different from the reasonable part of mankind? Yet, if Christianity did not lend its name to stand in the gap, and to employ or divert these humours, they must of necessity be spent in contraventions to the laws of the land, and disturbance of the public peace. There is a portion of enthusiasm assigned to every nation, which, if it hath not proper objects to work on, will burst out, and set all into a flame. If the quiet of a State can be bought by only flinging men a few ceremonies to devour, it is a purchase no wise man would refuse. Let the mastiffs amuse themselves about a sheep's skin stuffed with hay, provided it will keep them from worrying the flock. The institution of convents abroad seems in one point a strain of great wisdom, there being few irregularities in human passions which may not have recourse to vent themselves in some of those orders, which are so many retreats for the speculative, the melancholy, the proud, the silent, the politic, and the morose, to spend themselves, and evaporate the noxious particles; for each of whom we in this island are forced to provide a several sect of religion to keep them quiet; and whenever Christianity shall be abolished, the Legislature must find some other expedient to employ and entertain them. For what imports it how large a gate you open, if there will be always left a number who place a pride and a merit in not coming in?

Having thus considered the most important objections against Christianity, and the chief advantages proposed by the abolishing thereof, I shall now, with equal deference and submission to wiser judgments, as before, proceed to mention a few inconveniences that may happen if the Gospel should be repealed, which, perhaps, the projectors may not have sufficiently considered.

And first, I am very sensible how much the gentlemen of wit and pleasure are apt to murmur, and be choked at the sight of so many daggle-tailed parsons that happen to fall in their way, and offend their eyes; but at the same time, these wise reformers do not consider what an advantage and felicity it is for great wits to be always provided with objects of scorn and contempt, in order to exercise and improve their talents, and divert their spleen from falling on each other, or on themselves, especially when all this may be done without the least imaginable danger to their persons.

And to urge another argument of a parallel nature: if Christianity were once abolished, how could the Freethinkers, the strong reasoners, and the men of profound learning be able to find another subject so calculated in all points whereon to display their abilities? What wonderful productions of wit should we be deprived of from those whose genius, by continual practice, hath been wholly turned upon raillery and invectives against religion, and would therefore never be able to shine or distinguish themselves upon any other subject? We are daily complaining of the great decline of wit among as, and would we take away the greatest, perhaps the only topic we have left? Who would ever have suspected Asgil for a wit, or Toland for a philosopher, if the inexhaustible stock of Christianity had not been at hand to provide them with materials? What other subject through all art or nature could have produced Tindal for a profound author, or furnished him with readers? It is the wise choice of the subject that alone adorns and distinguishes the writer. For had a hundred such pens as these been employed on the side of religion, they would have immediately sunk into silence and oblivion.

Nor do I think it wholly groundless, or my fears altogether imaginary, that the abolishing of Christianity may perhaps bring the Church in danger, or at least put the Senate to the trouble of another securing vote. I desire I may not be mistaken; I am far from presuming to affirm or think that the Church is in danger at present, or as things now stand; but we know not how soon it may be so when the Christian religion is repealed. As plausible as this project seems, there may be a dangerous design lurk under it. Nothing can be more notorious than that the Atheists, Deists, Socinians, Anti-Trinitarians, and other subdivisions of Freethinkers, are persons of little zeal for the present ecclesiastical establishment: their declared opinion is for repealing the sacramental test; they are very indifferent with regard to ceremonies; nor do they hold the JUS DIVINUM of episcopacy: therefore they may be intended as one politic step towards altering the constitution of the Church established, and setting up Presbytery in the stead, which I leave to be further considered by those at the helm.

In the last place, I think nothing can be plainer, than that by this expedient we shall run into the evil we chiefly pretend to avoid; and that the abolishment of the Christian religion will be the readiest course we can take to introduce Popery. And I am the more inclined to this opinion because we know it has been the constant practice of the Jesuits to send over emissaries, with instructions to personate themselves members of the several prevailing sects amongst us. So it is recorded that they have at sundry times appeared in the guise of Presbyterians, Anabaptists, Independents, and Quakers, according as any of these were most in credit; so, since the fashion hath been taken up of exploding religion, the Popish missionaries have not been wanting to mix with the Freethinkers; among whom Toland, the great oracle of the Anti-Christians, is an Irish priest, the son of an Irish priest; and the most learned and ingenious author of a book called the "Rights of the Christian Church," was in a proper juncture reconciled to the Romish faith, whose true son, as appears by a hundred passages in his treatise, he still continues. Perhaps I could add some others to the number; but the fact is beyond dispute, and the reasoning they proceed by is right: for supposing Christianity to be extinguished the people will never he at ease till they find out some other method of worship, which will as infallibly produce superstition as this will end in Popery.

And therefore, if, notwithstanding all I have said, it still be thought necessary to have a Bill brought in for repealing Christianity, I would humbly offer an amendment, that instead of the word Christianity may be put religion in general, which I conceive will much better answer all the good ends proposed by the projectors of it. For as long as we leave in being a God and His Providence, with all the necessary consequences which curious and inquisitive men will be apt to draw from such promises, we do not strike at the root of the evil, though we should ever so effectually annihilate the present scheme of the Gospel; for of what use is freedom of thought if it will not produce freedom of action, which is the sole end, how remote soever in appearance, of all objections against Christianity? and therefore, the Freethinkers consider it as a sort of edifice, wherein all the parts have such a mutual dependence on each other, that if you happen to pull out one single nail, the whole fabric must fall to the ground. This was happily expressed by him who had heard of a text brought for proof of the Trinity, which in an ancient manuscript was differently read; he thereupon immediately took the hint, and by a sudden deduction of a long Sorites, most logically concluded: why, if it be as you say, I may safely drink on, and defy the parson. From which, and many the like instances easy to be produced, I think nothing can be more manifest than that the quarrel is not against any particular points of hard digestion in the Christian system, but against religion in general, which, by laying restraints on human nature, is supposed the great enemy to the freedom of thought and action.

Upon the whole, if it shall still be thought for the benefit of Church and State that Christianity be abolished, I conceive, however, it may be more convenient to defer the execution to a time of peace, and not venture in this conjuncture to disoblige our allies, who, as it falls out, are all Christians, and many of them, by the prejudices of their education, so bigoted as to place a sort of pride in the appellation. If, upon being rejected by them, we are to trust to an alliance with the Turk, we shall find ourselves much deceived; for, as he is too remote, and generally engaged in war with the Persian emperor, so his people would be more scandalized at our infidelity than our Christian neighbors. For they are not only strict observers of religions worship, but what is worse, believe a God; which is more than is required of us, even while we preserve the name of Christians.

To conclude, whatever some may think of the great advantages to trade by this favorite scheme, I do very much apprehend that in six months' time after the Act is passed for the extirpation of the Gospel, the Bank and East India stock may fall at least one per cent. And since that is fifty times more than ever the wisdom of our age thought fit to venture for the preservation of Christianity, there is no reason we should be at so great a loss merely for the sake of destroying it.

"I saw the graves give up their dead."

The Day of Judgement

by Jonathan Swift

1731

With a whirl of thought oppressed

I sink from reverie to rest.

An horrid vision seized my head,

I saw the graves give up their dead.

Jove, armed with terrors, burst the skies,

And thunder roars, and lightning flies!

Amazed, confused, its fate unknown,

The world stands trembling at his throne.

While each pale sinner hangs his head,

Jove, nodding, shook the Heavens, and said,

'Offending race of human kind,

SWIFT / PRUDHOMME

By nature, reason, learning, blind;

You who through frailty stepped aside,

And you who never fell - through pride;

You who in different sects have shammed,

And come to see each other damned;

(So some folks told you, but they knew

No more of Jove's designs than you):

The world's mad business now is o'er,

And I resent these pranks no more.

I to such blockheads set my wit!

I damn such fools! - Go, go, you're bit.'

A

Modern

Proposal

(and other related brief works)

by

Abel

Prudhomme

"Yes, at last, we will be able to fling open wide our borders, and leave our walls unattended."

A MODERN PROPOSAL

For what to do with illegal immigrants, welfare recipients, and the reproduction of their children.

Appeals for charity continue to flood our airwaves. Our entertainments and well deserved pleasures are ceaselessly interrupted by videos, photos, and sound bites of starving children, and their backward mothers. We are harassed in our saunas, hounded in our gyms, and harried from the seclusion of our well kept homes. Even harder to bare or believe, we are pled upon to perpetuate the very minority masses presently seeking to crowd into our great way of life. And so, from the lower class communities surrounding us, to the illegal inroads at our nation's border, we are threatened with the disorganization of our much enlightened society.

Who, in fact, in this generation, or the one preceding it can deny that their own mind has been veritably stuffed with images of distended infant bellies, and dark bony female cheeks. Visions heaped upon us since the dawn of television, until rather than prevent them, the shutting of the eyes center them clumsily into the midst of our life, our liberty, and the pursuit of our happiness!

Who then shall rid us from these dark sights and from the

thematic cry that, with the voice of our own mothers, intrudes upon every bar and table with the chant, "remember the starving children!" Such deliverance is overdue, and I am sure would have come long ago had intellects great enough to do so sufficiently considered the fame that may be afforded them for solving so bothersome a dilemma. Yes, such a person would be lauded in this world with media attention and accolades equaling that of our most sexually promiscuous Hollywood star.

But I am not merely seeking to form some new avenue of mental health, nor do I attempt to offer an addition to the already too numerous collections of self-help books, that give no help at all. No, what I have to say here encompasses that which shall be found beneficial first to every infant, child, and adult living within our nation, and then to all beyond in what we still pronounce to be our planet Earth.

The solution I offer springs from no new well of thought. Neither is it an idea with roots outside of our own history, and nearby epoch of time. What I am about to suggest was submitted to the British elite over three hundred years ago by no less a personage than Jonathan Swift, outspoken voice of the Eighteenth Century, and world renown author of that great satire, Gulliver's Travels. Furthermore, as I shall shortly demonstrate, these same ideas that I present here have been successfully enjoyed by various social orders down through the annals of time.

As for myself, I have sat analyzing the matter for over two generations, as both the social and financial institutions of America have quietly proved themselves dysfunctional. Whether breaking up a family to produce a criminal turned extremist like Malcolm X, or following the perditious policies of a Greenspan and Rand, these methods have failed! Now, with frightening speed, we rush from a current state of recession towards a Second Great Financial Depression, the depths from which we may never return. So then, with the staple social reforms of the Twentieth Century facing imminent defunding, and the current administration running out of money, here is the question I wish to answer: "What will we do with the families of the increasingly unemployed lower classes, and with the growing flock of their new ally, the illegal immigrant?

Eat them! I shall not further tax the modern mind whose literary abilities have so darkly devolved since the time of Swift's proposition. To the point then – we shall eat them! Certainly, as offered by Swift, we shall dine upon their children. Yet I move to also include their even more succulently matured adult members. This leaves us with a flexibility of usefulness, for if we find the primacy to become the systematic riddance of this segment of our society, then the culinary preparation of their children is to be our chief consumption. Ah, but if after launching our endeavors we discover that the newly created market for subhuman flesh proves both financially viable *and* delicious, then we shall more appropriately focus upon the curing, cooking, canning, distribution, and subsequent enjoyment of these meatier adult designates within our soon to be better fed republic.

Of course, as is typically the case, before reaping the benefits of a new investment, expenditures must be made. How very fortunate then is the diametric opposition resulting from the execution of this plan, as one outlay of cost is replaced by another. Yes, fortified fencing, and strategically placed law enforcement agents *will* be needed to prevent unwilling members from removing themselves from these neighboring communities turned into food source. Yet such will no longer be the case at our national borders! Patrol agents may then be reassigned to maintain our new profits, and corral new arrivals into our nation's slums and barrios where they belong.

Yes, at last, we will be able to fling wide our borders, and leave our walls unattended. Immigrants will be encouraged to arrive in droves: their children welcomed as a choice delicacy, their women bred, and their men made available to our butchers for immediate sale at the local supermarket. Even the escaped criminal and deported prisoner will find themselves to be most desirable, as it has been reported in historical accounts that these tend to yield the more sumptuous taste of a well salted pig.

Naturally, there will be those among us who vehemently oppose this plan. To them may be offered psychological counseling, and seminar attendance to help gain rational enlightenment. For in casting off our Christian roots, and increasingly embracing paganism, we have set ourselves upon a path whose conclusion can only be both infantile and adult cannibalism.

A form of this, upon every continent of the planet, has been done before! In Asia, for example, a child was sacrificed every day to a prominent Hindu deity. The bodies of children in Europe, also used in the construction of buildings, were sacrificed once a year on what we now call Halloween. Australian cannibals, following a system closer to what I am suggesting, consumed parts of the human body for the particular improvement of its citizenry. And here, in both North and South America, among the indigenous people whose ancient culture we now so revere, the availability of human flesh was plentiful, thanks to regular sacrifices of sometimes thousands per day! All this would have continued until now, had it not been for the overbearing interference, and establishment of Christianity! Now, with these unwanted influences waning in our society, we are geared to return to a more modern and orderly use of human flesh.

Wars also must be anticipated, with nations too weak to likewise bring the treatment of their non-elite to its logical conclusion. Yes, and let them pour into the jaws of our increased military might: against our already superior weaponry, and the protein enriched power of our more muscular troops. For unlike the Empire of Great Britain at its height, we *will* know what to do with the darkly hued indigenous residents of our conquest.

So then, let us move forward to where a nation must go that has both denied its children the right to pray in public schools, and refused its infants the right to life for half a century! Let us no more tip toe towards the darkness, but let the lights be adjusted now!

And why not free ourselves from the shackles of hypocrisy, and make gain of our present paganistic tendencies? Since 1973, over 50,000,000 infants have been slaughtered within or directly after being taken from their mother's womb! A mounting number of deaths occur daily among immigrants trekking to and through our national borders! And gunned down inner city victims of homicide are bled, boxed, and buried with no garner of assistance being rendered to our much needed health, and economy! Think of it then, as you now should. Creamy pate upon crackers, gobs of well seasoned meat lifted atop silvery platters; riches in our pockets; and yes, more jobs for the lesser than affluent of our people; all gained by the recaptured expenditure of human loss.

"Give me your tired, your poor, your huddled masses," was once part of a motto not merely carved into a plaque, found within the base of a statue in New York Bay. These were words our nation lived by, until we began our current wasteful discard of the unborn, and our resistance to needy families begging for entrance into, and participation within our world. Now, with the implementation of this proposal, we will once again be able to say with an honest heart, "Let the downtrodden come in!"

And what, someone might say; will we do if ever this newfound foreign and urban delicacy becomes extinct? Well, as we learned in our former mishandlings of the unwanted unborn… there are always *our own children!*

*"The President's a black man now,
Harrah! Harrah!"*

A Civil Rights Anthem
(hauntingly sung to the tune of "When Johnny Comes Marching Home")

Oh, Civil Rights is over now, Harrah! Harrah!
They don't hang us on trees no more, Harrah! Harrah!
They harass my family, lock up my sons,
Point at my suit with their loaded guns;
But they say it's over... Civil Rights is over, now!

Oh, Civil Rights is over now, Harrah! Harrah!
They gave us what we wanted now, Harrah! Harrah!
All our leaders who stood up got shot in the back,
And the ones who remain now all sit in their lap,
And tell us it's over. Civil Rights is over now!

Oh, Civil Rights is over now, Harrah! Harrah!
They tell me that it's over now, Harrah! Harrah!
So I'm off to work where they're telling me
To be a good boy at these jobs: all three...
Are you sure it's over? Civil Rights is over, now!

Oh, Civil Rights is over now, Harrah! Harrah!
The President's a black man now, Harrah! Harrah!
All their clinics are open, our daughters are there,
Our babies are murdered, our playgrounds are bare,
But he says its over! Civil Rights is over, now!

"We don't want the word to go out that we want to exterminate the Negro population, and the minister is the man who can straighten out that idea if it ever occurs to any of their more rebellious members."

Proposal #1:
End the Death Camps

Revealing the need to end the Great American Holocaust which quietly began after the abandonment of Reconstruction.

My subject for this first proposition, startling though it may be, is the genocide (removal by death) of the American people. It is my intention to awaken you to the history, current existence, and future results of this suicidal atrocity. In the end, you may walk away believing that this was just another proposition given by a black man speaking about black people, or African-Americans, or Negroes, or whatever else you wish to call... *us*. But what I am about to tell you cannot be considered to pertain to one so called "race".

This is the 21st century, and the modern anthropologist has confirmed what the conscience of everyman has dictated since the morning Adam woke to find Eve laying beside him: we are all of one race, the human race. And so I come to you representing not some newfound alien species, nor only those living at the lower ends of our society. No, tonight I represent... *you*!

Genocide is reaching for *your* door. Aye, for the blood of over a million Armenians starved to death by the Turks - mingles with that of 300,000 Chinese raped and massacred by the Japanese - joins the stream of 6 million Jews, a ½ million Gypsies, and 70,000 others "exterminated" by the Germans – increases as a crimson flood through the 1 ½ million Cambodians slaughtered by the communist Khmer Rouge – is screamed into a river by the bloody voices of 800,000 Tutsis bludgeoned and hacked to death in the streets of Rwanda... and is America clean? This, your last question, as a new Red Sea... of blood... rises up like a tsunami to gobble you from the porch you should have stepped off of long, long ago. And the quote floats through your mind, as you gasp for your last cup of breath: John Donne whispering, "No man is an island entire of itself."

So now, while you still may, remove your fingers from your ears and hear...

Where American Genocide Began

In 1863, President Lincoln freed the slaves by signing the Emancipation Proclamation. Reconstruction followed, from the middle of the Civil War until 1877, in which blacks were helped to acquire both education and employment. Then, suddenly, fearing that 4 million newly freed blacks would choke the economy, a movement known as Colonization attempted to send them all back to an Africa they had never known. This failed, and in 1883, Francis Galton invented the term eugenics and helped to found the movement by the same name. Galton defined eugenics as, "The ideal of perfecting the human race by getting rid of its undesirables while multiplying its desirables."

Galton was largely influenced by his cousin, Charles Darwin, founder of the theory of evolution, whose racial views can be summed up in the following quote from his book, "The Descent of Man, and In Relation to Sex", published in 1871, "At some future period, not very distant... the civilized races of man will almost certainly exterminate, and replace, the savage races throughout the world." He then went on to speak of the comparative inferiority of the "baboon... the Negro... [the] Australian and the gorilla."

Then the eugenics movement picked up steam and began to promote *positive eugenics,* where the white population would have so many children that they would overwhelm the others. When this failed, their tactics switched to *negative eugenics,* in which colored races are aggressively discouraged from giving birth. Margaret Sanger then spearheaded this forceful movement after founding the American Birth Control League, which after a failed attempt to merge with the American Eugenics Society, later changed its name to Planned Parenthood..

The following (one of many such quotes) is taken from a letter that Margaret Sanger wrote to Dr. Clarence Gamble on December 19, 1939. It is available for viewing online at JonesReport.com, in an article given by Aaron Dykes, and entitled, "Eugenics Quotes: From Lofty Ideals to Highly-Centralized Population Control Run by Psychopathic Maniacs": "We should hire three or four colored ministers, preferably with social-service backgrounds, and with engaging personalities. The most successful educational approach to the Negro is through a religious appeal. We don't want the word to go out that we want to exterminate the Negro population, and the minister is the man who can straighten out that idea if it ever occurs to any of their more rebellious members."

Genocide, genocide, genocide! You have heard... do you now dare see? Then, secondly, remove your hands from your eyes and see...

Where American Genocide Is Today.

The streets are empty. Like phantom memories from years gone by *(or are those the ghosts of the murdered dead?),* my ear seems to hear the laughing voices of children... but they are not there. The wealthy elite have surgically removed them from our midst.

According to "Table 101"of the U.S. Census Bureau, the total amount of children lost to family planning between the years 2000 and 2005 was an average of 1,247,097 children each year; and a comparison from "Table 99" of data occurring between 1990 and

2005 show an average of 482,000 black babies "eliminated" annually during that fifteen year period alone, along with 801,000 white infants, and 83,000 of other races.

Where are the children of America? Studies report that the total black babies lost to "family planning" is higher than the total of people who died in the Vietnam War. Where are the children? Strollers remain on the shelves in cities like Brentwood and Pasadena, while dog leashes sell out. Where are your children? The sight of a young child brings increasingly larger-sized crowds to doddle and gape, and no one wonders why?

So, since no one seems to be responding to these questions, let's let Sir Julian Huxley, Planned Parenthood honoree, give his answer, as quoted in Life Dynamics Incorporated's shocking 2009 video documentary, "Maafa 21: Black Genocide in 21st Century America": "They must not have too easy access to relief or hospital treatment, lest the removal of the last check on natural selection should make it too easy for children to be produced or to survive."

Genocide, genocide! Here in America. Do you begin to see? Then take your hand from your mouth and be ready to speak after I lastly reveal...

Where American Genocide Will End

Lets revisit those Census figures we quoted earlier. From between the years 1990 and 2005, there are at least 12,811,000 white children who are not here thanks to the backfire of the "non-white" extermination efforts of Sanger, Darwin, Hitler and others. And do you think it's over? Think again.

"White Supremacist Websites Foster Hatred", an article written by Richard Firstman, in 2004, which was printed in Opposing Viewpoints: Hate Groups, says, "The greatest source for Nazi material in Germany today is the United States." And you think that genocide in America is over? Think again.

Yes, in attempting to eliminate another race - that gave its blood, sweat and children to keep the white American family clothed and comfortable - in committing genocide upon a populace that should have been nurtured, cared for, and made into a viable participatory member of their society - in committing national mass murder, the elite white supremacists of this nation are smashing the heads, burning, ripping out the limbs, and slitting the throats of 21,856,000 children every 15 years, the bulk of which... are their own.

The August 12, 1996 edition of US News and World Report, gives figures from Planned Parenthood's own research division, the Alan Guttmacher Institute, which reports that "Blacks ... have 31% of all abortions and whites... have 61%". And so I ask you... who is killing who?

Conclusion

I have now exposed the history, existence and future... of the blood flowing in our streets. Genocide! I have backed up this revelation with solid data, historical facts, and irrefutable statistics. Never forget! Whether you rise up into the top ranks of society, or remain a dedicated member of its lower end, commit to fight against this nightmare living outside your walls.

And one last word...

Because of the brevity allotted to me for this discussion, as I spoke, I held close a bulging Pandora's box of related modern day ills, such as today's headlines concerning the genocide in Darfur, and the state of Arizona's eugenicist-like handling of its so-called "illegal immigrants". Yet concerning the latter, let me leave you with this one bit of common sense. It is not because they are illegal, nor because of anyone's concern with migration that these poor people in our society are hounded by so-called "Americans". That is an intellectual excuse that masks an overly charged emotional response. No! It is because they are... Hispanics! So stop calling them "Illegals": the same tactic used in the previous century of phrasing the poor and blacks as "feebleminded." Instead, I call you to stand up, like a true American, and help these new Americans to assimilate into our society. And if you don't... then you are the very person I have been speaking against... tonight.

"And seven children had to die, ..."

How Much Does a Planet Cost?

Save a penny, save a dime!
Buy organic? Not this time.
Boycott Gap, but then you fail.
The jeans you bought you bought on sale.

A worker had to lose his hand,
To make that handbag in your hand,
And seven children had to die,
So you could have a shiny tie.

But it's ok, you business man,
You lady with a budget plan,
You cut the cost and lost the Earth,
But look how much your worth!

"Most 'hungry countries' have enough food for all their people right now…"

Proposal #2:

End Global Suicide

A call to the next generation to bypass their elders, unify their efforts and bring a true and final end to the ongoing destruction of their planet.

Who could not weep when considering the future of humankind on Earth? Those who surround themselves with the comforts and privileges of today's elite? Those detached from the dusty scuffle of billions suffering amidst societal decay and physical depravation? Or most certainly those who do *not* tuck a child in at night, kiss that rosy cheek, and then contend with an honest heart that cannot cease to break when considering the swirl of unrest that they shall send this tiny mite into!

It is common knowledge that our planet is currently undergoing a rapid decline in its ability to sustain itself into the future. Of course, reports of this usually present either little to no hope for improvement or, as is more often the case, a lopsided view geared towards the prospect of personal gain for both the informant and those she or he represents. The purpose of this proposal is to provide the reader with certain points of information which may direct towards a realistic outlook for a sensible joint existence between our progeny and their inherited planet of residence, Earth.

I appreciate the honesty of Robert B. Laughlin. Mr. Laughlin is an accomplished scientist who, in 1998, received a Nobel Prize for his work in Physics. In his new book, *Powering the Future,* he utilizes his abilities to step out of the realm of fact and into the field of prophetic projection. More simply stated he attempts to predict the future. In doing so, he takes what he correctly calls "an armchair journey into the distant future" (1). This is accurately phrased, and is, in fact, the same type of journey taken by many elite thinkers writing before him.

Of course, the basic problem with such literary time travel is that these premier conceptualists, in most cases, remain within the sleek comforts of their "armchair", sipping tea and, as in the case of Laughlin, explaining away concern with such statements as, "Slowing man-made extinction in a meaningful way would require drastically reducing the world's human population. For better or worse, that is unlikely to happen" (Laughlin 10). Meanwhile, the next generation of caretakers, spawned from the Garden of Eden, is left befuddled and contending with feelings of isolation as they receive the product of ecological mishandlings passed on to them by the present guardians signing off from their shift for the night.

Yet one must not be too harsh towards this inconsistency in understanding. It is, after all, a common tendency in human nature. A person with a one sufficient source of income tells another forced to work three jobs, "Simply do the math and get one that pays the same as three." A governor in Arizona, with pearls wrapped around her neck, cannot grasp the burden propelling an illiterate mother to "illegally" transcend heavily guarded state and national borders to feed children she is forced to never see again. In the next few pages, an attempt will be made to both take a closer look at the issues demanding attention in today's global environment, and to then move beyond such fallibility in reasoning, and into carving out a path towards a world that works!

To address *all* the concerns needing such attention would take volumes far beyond the scope of this brief article. However, finding a starting point to be necessary, one may begin by witnessing the ravenous gulps of both creature life and human culture rapidly occurring every day. This concern has been referred to as "extinction debt", in author Terry Glavin's book, *The Sixth Extinction*. He defines this as the eventual loss of vast segments within a given species, particularly in areas that have been ravaged by ecological disasters, such as deforestation. In some cases, Glavin points out, "It might take a century" for a system of species to be lost, "but", as he goes on to say, "the debt will be called, and it will be paid" (21). Whole groups of species necessary to the Earth's inter connective chain of survival simultaneously lost forever. Animals only? No, entire cultures of civilization and human ability disappear right alongside the uncared for brute beast. But the tea is still sipped, and the "armchair" still feels good.

Yes, many will want to write such doom saying off as not *really* applying to mankind itself. Further investigation however will reveal that this is just not the case. As Paul Hawken brings out in his excellent work, *The Ecology of Commerce*, "Literally thousands of native cultures around the world have been destroyed by economic development." He then lists some of the major losses within these cultures being "languages, art and craft, family structures, land claims, traditional methods of healing and nourishment, rites and oral histories" (136).

Realities such as this and more may lead one to believe the situation to be irreversible. Fortunately, sufficiently conducted research shows that, in unearthing each particular problem, we may also discover the very tools needed for resolution.

One commonly understood answer to the ecological plight facing us today is the fact that better power sources do presently exist. As stated in a popular varsity press text entitled, *Physical Geography, a Landscape Appreciation*, "The harnessing of energy from sunlight, tide, and wind... are particularly attractive resources because they are free, renewable, clean, and virtually unlimited" (McKnight 113).

Yet, as Hawken puts it, "an even closer search for answers may be found right alongside the very problems themselves" (136). When it is understood how blatantly they are *not* being utilized, just *how* close such answers may be is almost frightening.

For a clear depiction of this, we turn to what many consider to be the premier work on the subject of global hunger. *World Hunger: 12 Myths* is an extremely well documented book, which is now in its second edition. The three authors, Frances Moore Lappe, Joseph Collins and Peter Rosset pull from heavily researched data, gathered from reams of research conducted by the Institute for Food and Development Policy (Food First). This work irrefutably debunks 12 popular misconceptions for the origins of hunger throughout the world. The very first such "myth" stripped away is that *there's simply not enough food in the world to sustain the current global population*. The following is an extended quote from this extremely relevant first chapter.

Most 'hungry countries' have enough food for all their people right now...

> 1. India ranks near the top among third world agricultural exporters... while at least 200 million Indians go hungry.
> 2. Bangladesh's official yearly rice output... could provide each person with a pound of grain per day... yet the poorest third of the people in Bangladesh eat... dangerously below what is needed for a healthy life.
> 3. While Brazil exported more than $13 billion worth of food in 1994 (second among developing countries), 70 million Brazilians cannot afford enough to eat.
> 4. Sub-Saharan Africa, home to some 213 million chronically malnourished people (about 25 percent of the total in developing countries),

>continues to export food... casting doubt on the notion that there are simply too many people for scarce resources (8-14).

Thus, the misguided outcry for population control is so easily stifled. Thus, those so quick to propose the prevention or ending of infant human life are refuted and made ashamed. Thus is revealed the truth of the hunger problem facing mankind at this fateful hour in the history of their existence. It is not that there is too much human life on Earth. It is rather that there is too much greed in the world. Let the lie no more be addressed. There is plenty of food; whether it is being *shared* is the question!

Yes, perverted economics spawn the painful nuances of a perverted ecology. Yet see how clearly the illness stands close to and in front of the cure. So then, when we read statements like, "industrial economies have caused increased polarization of rich and poor" (Hawken 136), we naturally wonder - can such polarization be demagnetized? Yea, can the hidden truth be pulled out from behind the overbearing deception presently blocking the revelation of an answer so vitally needed?

In responding to these questions, the pocketbook of big business is always a good place to begin. Hawken and others constantly, and very wisely, point to this common sense starting point to correcting the current dysfunctional global economic system. But wait! Could it *really* be true that incentives appealing to financial greed are the only workable solutions to saving billions of people and the very planet they call home? Is human nature so base that the key to rescuing itself lies in offering it something as philosophically miniscule as *money*?

John D. Kasarda is the director of the Frank Hawkins Kenan Institute of Private Enterprise, which is a part of the business school of the University of North Carolina. As a Distinguished Professor of Strategy, he is a leading entrepreneur in the field of increasing corporate profit through innovative city planning. His book, *Aerotropolis: The Way We'll Live*, provides the business community with cutting edge knowledge for prospering in this present age of digital technology. Note carefully the last five words given in the following quote from his popular book: "The race to build the perfect biofuel is being run by small teams of biochemists and molecular engineers lured from their ivory towers by the promise of saving the world and owning the basic patents" (Kasarda 347).

Yes, for the love of money the business community has and will lift a finger to conclusively assist its fellow man. Whether in order to sell "the basic patents" or to make a profit from the use of sustainable strategies for commerce, down through history, financial leaders have proven the truth of that modern axiom, "Follow the money, honey!"

Leslie Christian, an investment fund manager, who is quoted in Michael Shuman's book, *Local Dollars, Local Sense,* insists that, "Without strong local and regional economies there can't be a long-term successful global economy." So then, in the new global commerce rapidly evolving today, it becomes apparent that replacing the current philosophy of exploitive economics with that of sustainability would indeed garner a greater financial return.

Another area to be considered is the selection and subsequent representation of our future civic leaders. In his excellently written book, *Swimming in Circles: Aquaculture and the End of Wild Oceans,* Paul Molyneaux shares a warning from Jim Anderson, a professor from the University of Rhode Island, regarding "governing institutions." According to Anderson, "if varying governments are unstable, unfair or corrupt, then sustainability is unlikely."

A reversal of fortune then *is* plausible. As Karl Weber has said in his now famous book, *Food, Inc: How Industrial Food Is Making Us Sicker, Fatter and Poorer; and What You Can Do about It: A Participant Guide,* "Once corporations… realize that businesses can derive big profits from cleaning up the planet and operating in green, sustainable ways, the battle will be won" (Weber 58). Still some experts believe that "we don't have the focus and persistence to take on something really big, where the benefits play out over the long term" (Friedman 7). Are they right? Fortunately, some by their actions disagree.

The youth of any given society is the genesis of hope for their future. Unfortunately, many take an adverse view of the current up and coming next generation. Yet, in taking a closer look, examples of success stories abound. One such example is given on Discovery Communications' website, Treehugger.com, where we find:

> A program that's thriving in St. Paul, Minnesota could serve as a model for success across urban America that could ignite a passion for going green among our inner city youth. Dedicated to the idea that urban youth can learn about sustainability while discovering potential new careers and making their portion of the world a greener and brighter space. (Luna)

Yes, despite many so called business professionals having written them off, inner city youth can be a great resource in building a sustainable framework for both the ecology and business practices of tomorrow. This of course applies to the youth of every varying strata of human society. So, with such an awakening vision viewed against the reality of a background plagued with great ecological problems, how may these new troops of tomorrow be utilized in a fight to recover their world?

We must point them in the direction of changing the world around them in a much more workable way than is presently practiced. Not just by recycling bottles, but by creating a sustainable community in the world *directly* around them, by demanding that the businesses serving them participate in practices that return the Earth to the necessary balances needed for a thriving existence, and lastly by applying group pressure upon those chosen to represent them within the leadership of local, state and national government.

Niki Walker is an author who has written many books geared towards educating the young adult population on issues involving the environment. In *Biomass: Fueling Change* she writes, "Getting people to replace fossil fuels with biomass will require planning, time, and money." She then goes on to provide us with the following account of where this proposal is actually being done. "In September 2005, Reynolds, Indiana, became the first town in the world to begin making the switch to bioenergy. ... The people of Reynolds hope to prove that energy needs can be met by using biomass." Ah, the people of Reynolds, who may "hope to prove" facts about bioenergy consumption, are *in fact* proving that the human psyche *does have* the capacity to save itself; fact not fiction (Walker 28-29).

The community of Reynolds then provides a working model ready to be duplicated. The young leaders in our communities, whether abiding in the cities, suburbs or countryside must band together and agree to follow this same pattern of commitment to sustainable energy usage. And, as a child abandoned in a burning house, they must no longer wait for the leaders of the previous century to direct them. They must now fight their way out together, separating from the lethargic older generations around them. Once this has been put into practice, with this working example thus imitated, and with the living leadership of the *real* future activated, how shall they next proceed?

Further action. Talks abound; books and articles, both in print and online, pile up into untold millions; and even video and other multimedia resources, while proving informative, often do no more than entertain and lull their audiences back to sleep. The time for a real response conducted with urgency in real time exists not in the near or "distant future", but rather now; right now today.

When Rosa Parks refused to stand up and give away her seat, she did something. When the people of Montgomery, Alabama subsequently boycotted the bus company in their community they did something. When Dr. Martin Luther King Jr. and others utilized the cutting edge media of that time to bring national attention to the abusive practices of the Jim Crow South *they did something;* something that others had only talked and dreamed of doing. They brought down an age old system and accomplished in a few years what would have taken centuries to do had-they-*not-done-something!*

Now today's progeny must refuse to stand aside and give away their world. Companies not willing to perform their businesses in a way that truly engenders a sustainable environment must be openly boycotted. This of course includes the eradication of smoke and mirror tactics insultingly geared to deceive consumers into perceiving companies to be sustainable when they are not. And to do this, will the busy youth of America need to leave the comfort of their homes, and the stations of their schools and workplaces? Not necessarily.

The Digital Divide: Arguments for and Against Facebook, Google, Texting, and the Age of Social Networking, is a must read for those wishing to have a better understanding of the present influence of social technology. This book, edited and introduced by Mark Bauerlein, features an array of commentary from prominent intellectuals with a working understanding of the social media in force today. This book opens by dividing the world into two groups. The second group, labeled "social immigrants" is said to be those born before 1980 and thus raised without a life long use of today's media technology. However, the second group, "social natives" *have* been wired, almost from birth, with highly honed abilities in social technology ranging from a mastery in the usage of email, Facebook, Twitter, Google, Wikipedia, texting, and the abundant set of devises that now make these social medium virtually accessible anyplace and at anytime (Bauerlein 14).

These "social natives" continually demonstrate that they are a force to be reckoned with. Such power can be exemplified through the rapid speed in which information is now dispersed and responded to by an audience of unimaginable proportions. For example, one of the many statistics given in the work presented by Bauerlein and others is that within a span of thirty days only, during April, 2009, "Americans spent… 13,872,640,000 minutes" on Facebook. That's almost 14 trillion minutes. Doing the math on this statistic will leave one's mind boggled to discover that this equates to an average of every person living in the U.S. spending over 48 ½ days during a time span of only 30 days on this one social network alone.

Therefore, the tools of protest to either alter or topple entities poisoning our environment are presently humming and ready to be used. The warmth of these weapons of protest are felt atop almost every desk, within almost every bag or backpack, and within the ever close proximity of nearly every pocket of those born before 1980. Thus the great call to arms in the birth of our nation, and the appeals to march during the Civil Rights Movement of the previous century, may now, at the dawn of this new Millennium be simply equated to "lift every phone and text, and then comply!" Comply with what you tell and hear until first this great nation, and then this great world has been altered forever for good… again!

Although, it would be fitting to end this challenge to America's youth here, yet one last brief direction remains to be given. In 2008 the new social medium took the old world format of politics by storm. In an unprecedented move that left the established prognosticators breathlessly overwhelmed and dismayed, an unexpected winner was proclaimed in the presidential candidacy. Barack Obama became the first African-American president of the United States of America. Let therefore a new cry for freedom be raised up by the inheritors of this planet. "We texted you in, and we can text you out; beware because we can see what you are all about!" Social natives unite and know that your voice is amplified!

Works Cited

Bauerlein, Mark, Small Gary, and Vorgan Gigi. *The Digital Divide, Writings For And Against Facebook, Youtube, Texting, And The Age Of Social Networking.* New York: J P Tarcher, 2011. Print.

Friedman, Thomas L. *Hot, Flat, and Crowded: Why We Need a Green Revolution – And How It Can Renew America.* New York: Farrar, Straus and Giroux, 2008. Print.

Glavin, Terry. *The Sixth Extinction: Journeys among the Lost and Left Behind.* New York: Thomas Dunne Books, 2006. Print.

Hawken, Paul. *The Ecology of Commerce: A Declaration of Sustainability.* New York: HarperCollins, 1993. Print.

Kasarda, John D., and Greg Lindsay. *Aerotropolis: The Way We'll Live Next.* New York: Farrar, Straus and Giroux, 2011. Print.

Lappe, Frances, Joseph Collins, et al. *World Hunger: 12 Myths.* 2nd ed. New York: Grove Press, 1998. Print.

Laughlin, R. *Powering the Future.* New York, NY: Basic Books, 2011. Print.

Luna, Kenny. "Inner City Youth Discover Jobs, Sustainability, Green Spaces Through Ingenious Programs." *Treehugger, a Discovery Company.* 17 Sep. 2008. Discovery Communications, LLC. 22 Mar. 2012. Web.

McKnight, Tom Lee, and Darrel Hess. *Physical Geography, A Landscape Appreciation.* 9th ed. Upper Saddle River, NJ: Prentice Hall, 2008. Print.

Molyneaux, Paul. *Swimming In Circles: Aquaculture and the End of Wild Oceans.* New York: Thunder's Mouth Press, 2007. Print.

Shuman, Michael. *Local Dollars, Local Sense: How to Shift Your Money from Wall Street to Main Street and Achieve Real Prosperity.* White River Junction, VT: Chelsea Green Publishing Company, 2012. Print.

Walker, Nikki. *Biomass: Fueling Change.* New York: Crabtree Publishing Company, 2007. Print.

Weber, Karl, et al. *Food, Inc: How Industrial Food Is Making Us Sicker,*

Fatter and Poorer; and What You Can Do about It: A Participant Guide. New York: PublicAffairs, 2009. Print.

*"From Columbus crew
To parties of an elephant and ass."*

Her Khan

Her Khan would conquer

Land and love and life and liberate

Indigenous tribes established

From the petals of a mayflower

Blown apart by rocky shores of

Oh, those bloody conquistadors

Never found that fountain of their

Youth from Yellow Seas and

Oriental bees who hum with

Pollinated dust

Swelled on ancient thighs

Spreading bars of gold and black

And gold plucked from cotton kernels

Wet by blood that glistening

Sepia shaded colored

People offered salt and moisture

To a sun that saw no difference

Between the conquered and the conqueror

Save that one is driven mad

By the other

Then the other

By the other

Until know one knows

From where it all began

Except it is assured

That pounding feet

And beating hearts

And clenching fists

And gnashing teeth

From Columbus crew

To parties of an elephant and ass

Have filled the spacious mountaintops

With amber shades of gray

Leaving poisonous thrills

And oil spills

And Greenspan sea to see

Economy echo eat evaporate

And mark the ending beginning

The thing that put

Her Khan's foot

Back on the boat

That sailed away... home.

"England feared such light and the liberation its other colonies might gain from it. France attempted to grab hold of the fire and practically destroyed itself. What was the secret?"

Proposal #3: Wake Up!

America Personified

"The wicked shall be turned into Hell, and all the nations that forget God." ~ Psalm 9:17

Who are you? Are you the same person you were ten years ago? Are you the same person you will be tomorrow? And most of all, as you read this... who are you today?

As individualistic as we are, so too is a nation. It is, after all, the sum total of a group of *people*. Hitler's Germany had a persona; Mao's China has a persona; France, before during and after its revolution, had and has a persona; and so too does America.

This brief proposition is housed within the context of an emotionally charged perspective of our nation. With sincere heartfelt endeavor, an attempt will be made here to present an honest opinion on the America Persona in three parts: its childhood, its adult youth, and its present slippage into twilight. You may read the biblical quote provided above and draw your own conclusions as to what will be said if you wish, or you may read on. If you do so, please note that it will be sought, within each of the three proposed sections, to answer two simple questions. What did (or does, or will) this America have for its fellow nations; and what is there for you?

Who Was America?

When the nations of the world were of consenting age, there came forth upon the placenta of the vast connective oceans a cry of infancy. Ships made from life giving earth and life breathing trees carried small groups of living organisms from the womb of these nations to the shores of a bright new world. Life loomed before these people filled with hope and opportunity.

As the single soul of one man or woman is deeply complex, so too were the combined desires and intents of those who came. Some sought to fulfill their greed of riches innumerable. Some reached forth into the light seeking freedom to worship God as they saw fit. Still others lifted their feet upon these wet shores to give answer to an indefinable urge to belong. All were distinct in their own way and yet all were alike in this: human depravity. Each brought with them into this new world a soul that was at once incomplete and corrupt, and in need of an infusion of life from God.

Societies were set up and, as with the variations in the cries of young toddlers, so too were the differences in their emphasis. While most simply settled in seeking to exist, some, like their mother countries, shopped their new environment for the wealth of its store. Then there were those who fought diligently for a close relationship with God as their Father. As with the art of a kindergarten class, none of these three groups were perfect in their creations. Lust, avarice, and even a small isolated incident of witch burnings in a tiny town called Salem; all would come to be eclipsed by those who chose to hearken unto the instruction of salvation found only through the Lord Jesus Christ. It was those who, with the dropping of tears and lifting up of heart rending prayers, painted the land with the backdrop of a great nation to come.

I. What was that America to others?

To the countries of the world there was peculiar regard for this rambling boy of the woods. They saw the vulnerability of inexperience and youth, and swam to rob, ransack, and ransom all they could. To most of them, this child was a fool cast aside by its mother and left to die upon a mountain of gold. Yea, to them we were but worthy in our ability to hand over treasure, and then worthless if we got in their way.

II. Who could that America have been to you?

One can but wonder what you would have done in such a place and at such a time. Would you have joined in with the groups of foreign and national plunderers? Yes, would you have come to take or to give? Would you have failed to seek beyond what you saw or would you have basked in the power of an America that had touched the hand of God? Would you then and do you now?

Who did America become?

The second half of the 18th century found a Europe not at rest. In the century prior, England had witnessed a successful rebellion that ended with the beheading of a king. In the century to come, France would likewise lop off the head of its majesty with much more crazed results. Enter into the middle of this the rising shoulders of America.

Strengthened in mind by its youthful resolves, its vastness of terrain, and by the bolstering floods of likeminded immigrants; it had grown like a young Alexander. With a strength and power yet to be tested, in its flesh lay the realities of human corruption. The betrayal and domination of a people who had once opened their doors as a trusting host; the selfish pursuits of land and wealth at any cost, including the slavery and brutal treatment of its fellow man; and worst of all, like a just judgment, its offspring had chosen to reject the pursuit of God for the ravening reasonings of a so called enlightenment.

Still, as there is a spirit in man so America owes the obtaining of its freedom to those who, through the Spirit of God, continued in prayer for the Almighty to make this nation great. Yes, the true "Spirit of '76 (1776) was the Holy Spirit of God.

And the answer did come; from the revival in England spearheaded by the Wesley brothers to their partner and friend George Whitefield carrying the torch to this continent, it came! Furthered by sermons like that of Jonathan Edward's reading[1] of "Sinners in the Hands of an Angry God", it came! An answer that mightily kept England from the death grasp of the irrational mob! An answer that delivered both us and the "mother country" from the permanent insanity inflicted upon its sister nation by the French Revolution. An answer that, in its over plus, would work to give us the Constitution, the Louisiana Purchase, and yea, even the thunder and lightning that, in our capitol, halted the advance of the returned oppressor during the War of 1812. Yes, all this from God *for* his people (and upon all fortunate to live among them) who, at this time, did worship him in "spirit and truth."[2]

I. What was this America to others?

Yes, in the middle of worldwide political unrest and ineffectiveness rose America; at first a land to be stolen from, then suddenly a land of shining liberty. England feared such light and the liberation its other colonies might gain from it. France attempted to grab hold of the fire and practically destroyed itself. What was the secret? God and no other.

---

[1] Yes, he simply read his pre-written sermon while holding a tray with a lighted candle in one hand and dropping page after page with the other. With God present this was all that was needed before people were grabbing onto pillars and crying out for mercy from God.

[2] John 4:24

As the Samaritan[3] who lay bleeding in Jesus parable so every nation lies abused by the acts of the sins of its people. If, in its persona, it allows for the intervention of God then like serum to the infirmed, revival of true religion will come. (And so to, like most of the sick, it cannot be understood how such medicine could help… yet, if balm is accepted, health will come.) With it a nation will flourish. America did and so too did England, when they both, as nations personified, did not reject God. Note that, on the contrary, France who both slew and cast out those who named the name of Christ… never prospered again!

II. Who could this America have been to you?

It is interesting to note that as the Great Awakening [Revival] occurred before the American Revolution so too the Second Great Awakening preceded the Civil War. During these times of spiritual plenty those usually too hardened to escape eternal judgment were swept easily into the Kingdom of God. Yet many "being often reproved [were] suddenly destroyed, and that without remedy."[4] And so in this section we ask simply, "Which one would you have been?

Who is America now?

*"How have the might fallen."*5

Behold the pompous fat businessman sitting in the plush chair of a continent, and surrounded by the comfort of two ocean views. He thinks himself invincible. He believes he is *the one* that all want to be and yes, *should* be. He is bald, he is fat, he is self-deceived into believing he can still play ball like he use to, and, although the warning signs are everywhere, he will soon be

---

[3] Luke 10:33

[4] Proverbs 29:1

[5] II Samuel 1: 27

shocked to find himself dying from a sudden heart attack.

Who is this person? You know who. It is America; or... was that you?

As in numerous historical accounts given in the Old Testament documenting man's rush to do so, the twentieth century watched as America rejected God and plummeted itself into the worship of idols. Many instances are historically recorded. We will only take time to mention three of the key occurrences that have brought this about.

First, in 1920, a people who wished to be rid of the reviving God of their parents and grandparents rushed en masse to become the radical believers of a new faith. Evolution, as it is falsely called, became the justification for everything from mass murder to the act of adultery. Next, in 1962 this people legally forbade their children from prayer to or even silent reflection of God during their many hours a day spent in school. Then, in 1973, they granted their children the legal right to crush, drown, starve and maim their unborn descendants; innocent little infants laying trustingly in the womb of their mothers. All this, and we wonder why they, these same children, almost burned this country to the ground in the insanity of the late 70s.

Having breathed in the flames we find it difficult to breath. We were taken off the field in stretchers and *body bags* from the jungles of Vietnam. We were brought back from the deserts of Iraq in pieces. Now, into another fight from which we may never escape, we find ourselves half way around the world scratching ourselves and asking, "Why are we here, again?"

And what of those of us back in the "office" here at home; too preoccupied to properly face consequences crowding in. We are broken financially; emptied morally, divided by the media, and made invalid by a technology that, whether held in hand or sitting somewhere nearby, *watches us* play out the end of a history once great.

I. Who is this America to others?

Our relationship to others on the global scene is varied. To some we are a partner whose great resources must be rendered first to help maintain their western control over the world. To others, we are a like a nuisance at parties, stepping on the shoes of the other guests; talking too much; and drunken with power. Still, to countless more "little" nations we are the rich aunt who is taking too long to die. After all, the inheritance is pending and the will (or is it "national debt") must be read, and the redistribution must commence as the world scene of history changes once again.

II. Who is this America to you?

To many immigrants we are the "golden mountain"... without gold. We are the land of opportunity – yet these opportunities are as unattained as they are undefined. We are the land that says, "Give me your tired and poor", and then locks the door and hunts them with dogs at our borders.

And what of you? Unless America returns to God we are worst than nothing to you. Nothing would be to leave you unaffected. Not so with modern day America. We suck away the bright face from your youth and fill your home with argument and confusion. We *are* the elite. *You* are the elite. You are an American from the day you wake up in this country (the right of legal due process proves it). And you have become a part of the end of a great dream. You are living the American nightmare!

The proposition? Well... can you wake up?

And now for…

A

Trilogy

of

Short

Satires

I
"The work order said it was here. Right here!"

II
"That boy… Stupid! That boy."

III
"It was six months after we arrived before I woke up."

I

Lyre, Lyre, Forest on Fire!
(a parable of the Lyre Bird)

"The work order said it was here. Right here! But every time I get this order, when we arrive, there's already a crew working the area."

Frank looked up from his desk at him. The smell of oil and smoke was fresh in the air. Bob always carried his chainsaw over his shoulder. Like a soldier and his rifle, it seemed to be a part of him, only instead of looking like it grew out of his shoulder blade, this thing seemed to extend from his hip.

"I'm sick of this, Frank," continued Bob, "My guys and I don't like wastin' our time like this. If you already got a crew, why do you keep sendin' us there? Each time we go, we wind up having to find another spot to clear."

"Calm down, Bobby! Sheesh, you'd think you and your guys could learn how to take advantage of these mix ups. I mean, if you get sent to the wrong place, why not just take it easy and enjoy a little nature that day. This *is* Brazil, you know? Lots to see out here!"

"There's nuthin' here," said Bob. "Nuthin' but a bunch o' creepy trees and weird animals! There ain't no bars, no theaters, no dames... there ain't even a descent channel to watch on TV! I hate this place! Why don't they just light a match and be done with it?"

"Bobby!" whispered Frank, "Don't talk like that! You know we ain't allowed to do that no more. Besides, the chief says they's makin' a lot o' money from all the wood we shippin' out. Gonna be some big bonuses come Decem---"

"Stop changin' the subject, Frank! Next week, when I get that same work order, like I know we'll get, *we're gonna saw right through that area, anyway!* And heaven help the fools you send in there ahead of us, 'cause there's gone be a lotta trees fallin' on their heads!"

One week passed, and sure enough, Bob and his crew got the same work order! Once again, when they arrived they could hear the other crew hard at work. This time, however, the other crew seemed to be moving away from them as their work continued; like they were walking while they worked.

"Those clowns are probably foolin' around in there," he told his foreman. "Betcha we'll get blamed for their mess, like the last time. Come on PeeWee! Get the guys! We're gonna walk in there and bust 'em, this time; and catch 'em right in the act!"

Bobby and his men tip toed in through the fresh foilage. Quietly coming closer and closer to the sound of the retreating saws. Yes, it wasn't until they began to step up over a ridge that they saw it. Loren, I'm tellin' you it was the strangest sight you'd ever wanna see. Ever!

Just over that ridge they saw...

Twenty or more big black peacocks running away into the deeper part of the forest; and right next to them, in groups running right alongside each large bird, was a bunch of little birds that looked like they had just gotten old enough to run too.

Bobby and the guys just stood there dumbstruck, with their mouths hangin' out! Not because of the bizarre scene they were facing. No, I suppose that would have been enough, but it wasn't that. It was the noise the birds were making as they ran away. The noise, the exact same noise, of a large professional team... of hacksaw workers.

Nature had finally spoke up!

Bobby and his guys never did tell Frank what happened; but from then on, whenever they got a work order where another crew seemed to be working, they would pull out their lunch boxes, have an all day picnic, and at least one of them would tell the new guy about the time they saw the sound of hacksaws running away!

The end. [We wish!]

II

What Was I Thinking?

An elderly woman, almost unnoticed, steps out of a worn, beaten up trailer, sets her aluminum folding chair in the shade, takes a seat, and more clearly now, remembers...

That boy... Stupid! That boy. He was so golden, and so shiny! Not like the pale dusty skinned ones back home. Stupid! It was only because of their star,

(Sarcastically)

with its heat, and life that gave them *color* – that gave them *death*. Killing me... *now!*

(Pause)

"Stay here until we return." Always looking for something, and me always in their way. I guess they were glad to get rid of me. Samples, collections, specimens; that should have been enough for me; enough to look at... Growing up with them staring me in the eye; dead, wet, staring at me, looking through the glass, with all the others, but never seeing me; invisible to everyone, *and* them.

I wanted one alive; wanted to meet one. Not the female, not the big ones; a boy; a golden shiny boy. And there he was; lying by all that water… but not in it; alive, skin so smooth and so real. I had to touch it, touch *him*, have him look at me, see me, want me, hold me, love me like they never could, never would, never did.

(Pause)

"We are our people's last hope. Our star fades, and something in their genetic code holds the answer." A little girl should not have to hear such things over and over again. They thought I was so *stupid*.

(Pause)

I am stupid! I followed that boy, and hid in his barn, until they flew away. Did they try to find me? I didn't care. I didn't want to be found. And so they flew away in the ship. Back to the dying world; back to the sunless people, back through the wormy "wormhole" in space; to the world they wanted to save, to the life they would happily lead, abducting specimens, *people* from worlds, and worlds far away; with no little girl to complain, and be constantly in their way. And so… I will die for a shiny golden boy who became – the dusty skinned man I buried last week. And here *I* sit, hidden from that other world, the alien who should have lived a thousand years, dying of *skin cancer*… in a week!

III

Save the Martians!

It was six months after we arrived before I woke up.

They were amazing. They had gone through all of our data; every inch of every application and every piece of software too. Productivity, math, education and especially entertainment; they had mastered it all... and they were a mess.

They had begun to argue and fight amongst themselves. Their formerly well organized family units began to dissolve, and their well kept society, which I later learned had lasted over ten thousand years, crumbled almost overnight!

All of my shipmates were dead, so they had waited. For six months they had carefully tended to me until I awoke. Hundreds of strange faces pressed in around me as one, like the multi-sectioned eye of a fly that couldn't blink. Green; nothing where a nose should be, eyes like black opals, and grins - a sea of smiles, of animal happiness that couldn't be rationalized through a lifetime of human corruption.

They spoke... spoke! English, and with no accent that I could perceive; amazing; and what did they want?

They wanted me to teach them the inner meaning of our world. Why were we the way we were? What was the purpose for all our organization if we just tore it all down through so many acts of violence, and why was so much of our time spent in that which benefited neither ourselves nor anyone else?

Morality, mission, meaning... I would have to instill all this in them, and quickly, if Mars was to survive this sudden interposition of... *our humanity!*

"A million deeds ungratifying, times ten thousand fears a-terrifying; multiplying, multiplying: Time is full."

Tree

AT A TIME WHEN ALL THINGS FIRST APPEARED,
BEFORE PROTRACTED PROGENY OF THOSE
TRUSTED TO PROTECT
RECEIVED PARENTAL DOSED ATTEMPT TO
UNCREATE CREATION'S TALE;
UPON THAT DAY THINGS FIRST ROOTED IN THE
GROUND
SPREAD INNUMERABLY DEEP AND DOWN,
UNTIL WHEN WITNESSED THEN OR VIEWING
NOW,
SEEMED JOINED UNTO WHAT WOULD BE
CALLED - THE LAND;

OF THOSE WITH BARK AND LIMB AND LEAF
AND LIFE
WHO TOUCHED THE SKY, COMPELLING PRAISE
UNTO THE ARTIST'S HAND,
FROM WHICH WHOLE JOY AND ENGINEERING
SCULPTURES WORKED WONDERS IN A WORLD

WHERE MANUFACTURED MATH DISPLAYED
EQUATION'S HEIGHT,
STOOD A TREE,

SEQUOIA TO BE CALLED ON HILLS BEYOND
THE SEA,
OF THICKEST BARK AND FIRMEST BRANCH AND
SAP THAT FLOWED TO EVERMORE ENDURE,
IT STOOD.

AND FROM A VANTAGE POINT WHICH THE
MOBILE WOULD REGRET,
THROUGH PATIENCE AND CONNECTION
UNDISCOVERED YET 'TWIXT
ALL COMPRISING BLUSH OF GREEN UPON THIS
PLANET'S FACE,
IT FIRST PERCEIVED.

THEN SOON BEHELD THE PLACING OF THE SUN
AND MOON AND STARS,
THEN SOON ENJOYED FIRST STANZA OF EACH
BIRD'S COMBINING SONG,
THEN SOON BEHELD THINGS WALKING, AND

FELT THE SHAKING OF ITS ROOT,
AND THEN... THE WORLD - WAS BENT UNTO A MAN.

YET THIS TREE AND ALL CREATION STILL DID SHINE,
AND COMMUNION'S UNBROKEN BOND DID STILL ABIDE;
AND ALL WAS WONDERFUL, AS THE LOVE THAT SOME NOW POSSESS BELONGED TO ALL,
AND ALL WAS AS IT WAS DESIGNED TO BE;

AND THEN… THE MAN-THING SINNED.

WHOSE DEVOLUTION THENCE COMMENCED,
AND ALMOST ENDED IN A FLOOD;
WHOSE INFECTING TOUCH OF CARE UNATTENDED ALWAYS CORRUPTS;
WHOSE DISSEMBLING WARS DISORGANIZE,
TAINT THE DIRT, AND MAR THE SKIES,
AND LEAVE A WORLD AGHAST... AT LOVE TURNED INTO GREED.

ALL THIS THE CENTER OF OUR TALE, MIGHTY
SEQUOIA DID DISCERN,
UPON A HILL AWAY FROM THOSE WHO DARE
TO CLIMB;
UNTIL THE YEARS BECAME SIX THOUSAND OF A
NEVER ENDING REACH,
UNTIL HE WHO WITHIN GREAT HEAVEN FAR
BEYOND THAT REACHED FOR SKY,
HE WHO WITH INFINITE WATCH DOTH SEE
AND HEAR AND KNOW AND FEEL AND GIVE
DID GRANT THE GIFT OF SPEECH UNTO THIS
ARBOR IN HIS ART;
'TIL THIS SEQUOIA OF THE AGES DID ENACT
THAT THING SO STRANGE;
AND SPOKE.

THERE HIGH STANDING LOOKING DOWN ON
HAIRLESS SKIN A SHADE OF BROWN
INTO ASIAN EYES THAT WOULD ONE DAY LOSE
THEIR SLANT,
YEA, LIKE A BROOK WHOSE BABBLE DOTH
FLOW FREE
THE TREE - UTTERED - THIS,

A MODEST PROPOSAL / A MODERN PROPOSAL

"MAN-THING, WHY COMEST THOU TO ME?"
AND ALL NATURE STILLED TO LISTEN QUIETLY.

THEN LIKE EVERYONE JUDGED IN OR SANE,
WHO HAD, OR DID, OR WILL,
INTERRUPTING COMMUNE OF MOISTENING
RAIN, AND BREATH OF WIND WHICH THRILLS,
WITH A SOUND THAT NATURE ONCE OBEYED
BUT NOW DOTH WISELY FEAR,
MAN-THING GAVE MAN-THING REPLY,
"O', TREE UPON THIS HILL, THOU ART MINE,
"AND ALL THE DIRT BENEATH MY FEET AND
AIR ABOVE MY HEAD
"EARNED IN THAT STRUGGLE THROUGH
THOSE STRAITS WHICH NOW POSSESS OUR
DEAD
"ALL THAT WHICH MY EYE BEHOLDS AND
WHICH MY MIND CAN SEE
"ALL THIS AND EVEN THEE, O' TREE BELONG
TO ME;
"THIS LAND IS MINE."

AND SO TOGETHER THE FOREST VOICE AROSE;

THE MOCKING BIRD, THE LAUGHING BROOK,
THE HOWLING WOLF, THE BEAR
GREW LOUD AND OVERWHELMED ENOUGH TO
FRIGHT THE FOOL,
WHO TOOK THE ONLY THING HE OWNED, HIS
SOUL AWAY FROM THERE,
HIS SOUL AWAY FROM THERE.

REPEAT REPEATED EXERCISE OF THIS, AND
MULTIPLY,
UNTIL THE PAST HAS PASSED AND DAYS
BECOME TODAY,
UNTIL THE PATIENCE OF THIS TREE AND ALL
OF NATURE DOTH COMBINE.
SIX THOUSAND YEARS:

CENTURIES AND CENTURIES OF ABNORMALITY
SEWN BY ROGUISH GARDENERS;
UNTIL PERNICIOUS PUTRID GODLESSNESS
PUTREFYING PETRIFIES INVASION
OF A WORLD THAT NOW APPROACHES WHAT IS
MORE THAN IT CAN BARE;
THAT VAIN MOCKERY WHICH WE DARE TO

CALL TOMORROW.

A MILLION DEEDS UNGRATIFYING, TIMES TEN
THOUSAND FEARS A-TERRIFYING
MULTIPLYING, MULTIPLYING:
TIME IS FULL.

NOW COMES THE ODDEST THING AGAIN,
NOT ONE TREE THIS TIME BUT ALL THAT
CRAWLS, OR RUNS, OR CLIMBS, OR SWIMS, OR
FLIES,
OR RISES UP OR DIGS INTO THE GROUND,
THAT IS OR ISN'T WHAT OUR EYES CAN SEE
OF ALL THE ELSE SURROUNDING WE, THE SELF
PROCLAIMED EVOLVED;

YOU COULD HEAR IT ON THE MOON,
KNEES DRAWN UP IN YOUR ARMS, EARS LIFTED
TOWARDS THAT PROPHESIZED TO COME:
THAT ONE LONG GROAN:
WHOLE CREATION TRAVAILED AND PAINED IN
LONGING
FOR THAT ONE TO COME

FOR WHOM ANGELIC VESSELS POURED OUT
ALL THEIR PRAISE
FOR WHOM THE HUMBLE AND THE PENITENT
FIND EXALTATION HERE AND THEN..

TWO THOUSAND YEARS AGO,
AND NOW, AND NOW, AND NOW, AND NOW...
THE DEAF RETURN TO SILENCE,
THE LISTENING FORGET AGAIN TO HEAR,
THEY WHO PREFER THE CACOPHONY LET THE
TRUTH FALL OFF THE EARTH
AND ARE LEFT FOR DOOM TO DRAW THEM TO
ITS ROOM.

AND YET THE HOPE, THE PROMISES ABIDE,
WHETHER REJECTED OR, IN VANITY NOT SEEN;
CHRIST WHO CAME BEFORE AS A COOING
CUDDLING CHILD
COMES AGAIN;

AND ROCKS, AND HILLS, AND EARTH, AND
SKIES, AND SEAS
... AND TREES

WILL SING THAT ANCIENT SONG WHICH THEY
HAVE GROANED SO VERY LONG TO SING,
AS THE EARTH WITH OR WITHOUT YOU SHALL
FILL ITSELF UP WITH
HIS PRAISE.

ABOUT THE AUTHORS

Jonathan Swift (1667 – 1745) was a graduate of Trinity College, Dublin (B.A., 1686). He was also a graduate of Hart Hall, Oxford (M.A., 1692). His Doctor of Divinity was much later received, in 1702, after having returned to Trinity College. Swift, who in his lifetime served as a priest, politician, poet, and pamphleteer, is best known as the greatest satirist in the English language. With almost a thousand pages of poetry, and at least fourteen volumes of printed prose, his two greatest works, both satires and both known all over the world, are Gulliver's Travels, and the one reprinted here, "A Modest Proposal."

Abel Prudhomme holds a degree in Biblical Studies from Louisiana Baptist University (B.A.). He is also a graduate of the Library Technology Program at Pasadena City College. His other published works (which are all available at Amazon.com) include "The Lost Canterbury Tale", 'and his newly released theatrical play, "Hamlet Resurrected", portions of which may be previewed via front page publication in the Fall 2012 online edition of West Magazine, or via a three part televised reading, from the "Spend a Little Time With Poetry Show", available on YouTube. More information, including his latest works and upcoming performances, is available at www.abelprudhomme.com.

WORKS BY ABEL PRUDHOMME

FICTION

THE LOST CANTERBURY TALE

NON-FICTION

A MODEST PROPOSAL/ A MODERN PROPOSAL

THEATRICAL PLAYS

HAMLET RESURRECTED

THE FRANKENSTEIN CHRONICLES

POETRY

I WILL HAUNT YOU

BOOKS ON TAPE

THE WAR – PART I: THE MAN

THE WAR – PART II: THE WOMAN

THE WAR – PART III: THE SAVIOR

CPSIA information can be obtained
at www.ICGtesting.com
Printed in the USA
FSOW02n2101220216
17255FS